Ghosts of the Sea Moon

Book One

Saga of the Outer Islands

A. F. Stewart

For all the secret swashbucklers and pirates.

And for all my fellow Genre Writers of Atlantic Canada that helped me with the nautical research.

More Books by A. F. Stewart

Fiction:

The Ghostly Tower (Heyward and Andersen #1)
Shadow in Scarlet (Heyward and Andersen #2)
The Headless Corpse(Heyward and Andersen #3)
Rivalry and Steam Monsters(Heyward and Andersen #4)
Eternal Myths
Past Legends
Ghosts of the Sea Moon (Saga of the Outer Islands Book I)
Souls of the Dark Sea (Saga of the Outer Islands Book II)
Renegades of the Lost Sea (Saga of the Outer Islands Book III)
Chronicles of the Undead
Killers and Demons
Killers and Demons II: They Return
Fairy Tale Fusion
Gothic Cavalcade
Ruined City

Multi-Author Anthologies:

Realms of Horror (Genre Writers of Atlantic Canada Book 2)
Realms of Fantasy (Genre Writers of Atlantic Canada Book 1)
Fairy Tales Punk'd
Cogs, Crowns, and Carriages
Hell's Empire: Tales of the Incursion
Abandon: 13 Tales of Impulse, Betrayal, Surrender, and Withdrawal
A Twist of Fate: A Collection of 11 Twisted Fairy Tales
Beyond the Wail
Legends and Lore
Mechanized Masterpieces
Christmas Lites Series (Books III-IX)

Poetry:

Roses and Ashes
Poetry of Monsters and Madness
Places of Poetry
Horror Haiku Pas de Deux
Horror Haiku and Other Poems
Colours of Poetry
Reflections of Poetry
Shadows of Poetry
Tears of Poetry

Raven Rock
Outcast Key
Silver Haven
Storm Point
Crakcrow Bay
Stone Fire Islands
Abersythe
Llansfoot
Temple of Star Reef
Evermarsh
Razor Reef
Pentown
Echo Bay
Black Shoals Harbour
Black Shoals
Red Bay
Crickwell Town
Crickwell Island
White Fin Point
Sunlight Bay
Bay of the Moon
Shadow Cay
Tenby Key
Riverford
Rock Island
Rock Island Temple
Old Town
Blue Bay
Deep Sea Key
Red Reef

Sea Portal
Mists of Infinity
Archipelago of Nightfall
Island of Stone
Ghastly Reef
Haven of Despair
The Isle of Bones
Ruins Key
Obscurity Atoll
Isle of Shadows
Mists of Infinity
Sanctuary of Shadows

Contents

Chapter One
The Captain

Captain Rafe Morrow paced the quarterdeck of his ship, *Celestial Jewel,* the signs of an oncoming squall setting him on edge. Blustering wind rattled the sails and the crew's nerves, their usual jaunty hubbub reduced to grumbling and snipes. Trouble travelled on that wind. Rafe could smell it woven in the air, and his blood prickled with a sense of worry. The ship trembled as if with warning. He glared at the sky and its darkening clouds painted amber and crimson from the setting sun. A storm sky coming ahead of a full moon meant dark magic and sea monsters would prowl the waves this night.

The Moon Goddess will hold sway tonight.

A trickle of blue energy raced across the back of his hand at the thought.

Damn her… and her beasts.

On the breath of a sigh, he whirled to face his crew.

"Storm's coming, boys. Doesn't bode well, not with the moonrise tonight."

"How long, Captain? Will we be in the thick of the weather or just what comes after?" A rough-edged sailor, Pinky Jasper, spoke up, but all ears of the deck crew listened for an answer.

"It's coming within an hour or two, out from Raven Rock, by my reckoning. After nightfall by certain. We're heading in, boys, but we'll likely hit the edge of it." He heaved a breath, exhaling. "It'll be a bad one even for this crew, so expect trouble."

A shiver of tension settled over the deck. Some of the crew cast worried glances at the sea and each other. Others shivered, and a few more whispered prayers. Storms brought bad memories and nervous anticipation to the sailors of this ship.

"Which port then, Captain?" The mariner at the ship's wheel chimed in. "Might make Abersythe if we head north."

"We might, Anders. But we head east. We'll race the edge of the tempest, but it's closer and the ship will find better shelter anchored at Crickwell Island."

"Aye, sir. Laying in course to Crickwell Island." One-Eyed Anders turned the wheel and the ship's bones groaned. Others of the crew adjusted the sails, and the *Celestial Jewel* leaned into her new bearing headed east.

The gusting wind caught across her now full sails, and she increased momentum. Fresh sea air swept through the deck amid grunts and swearing as the vessel lit alive with activity. The smell of ripe sweat mixed into the salt-stained air as the night stayed warm.

Rafe smiled at the sights, sounds, and smells. The comfort of a familiar scene. He laid a hand on the rail, whispering to his ship. From below deck, deep in the workings and bowels of the vessel, the ship's inherent magic blossomed into life. Energy quivered across wood and rudder, keel and mast, shuddering the ship into top sailing speed.

The race with the storm commenced.

Footsteps sounded behind the Captain, the scuff of stiff leather boots. "Something's brewing, isn't it?" The low, deep voice of the first mate drifted past Rafe's ear cast against the night wind. "There'll be creatures out tonight, but perhaps more than usual?" the first mate asked.

Rafe nodded, keeping his eyes towards the sea. "Another bad night, I fear, for some and for us, after. But we've handled worse, Blackthorne."

"Have we?" Blackthorne asked. "The air seems... different, I suppose. A change in the wind, if you will."

Rafe turned his head, surprised at the apprehension from his steadfast first mate. Behind him, Blackthorne stood ramrod straight, navy blue pea coat spic and span, tricorn hat perfectly in line, and clean shaven as usual. Yet, a wry and worried smile met Rafe's gaze.

"That's not like you, to say such things."

"I know, but I can't shake this sensation, a premonition

perhaps. I feel..." He let the sentence trail off before briskly adding, "Will we see the Moon Goddess tonight?"

The surprising question startled the captain, but, choosing to ignore his first mate's concerns, he shrugged and answered. "Perhaps. You never know when she'll leave her island. She's fickle, you know that. Odd of you to ask, though."

Blackthorne shrugged. "It's an odd night, I think."

Rafe gave him a smile, an unaccustomed tidbit of reassurance from captain to first mate. "Well, it is moonrise. You never can tell what life and the sea will bring on a moonlit evening. Perhaps you're right. Perhaps there will be a happening tonight."

Feet shuffled on deck, and Blackthorne stared toward the water. "I saw her for the first time when I was a lad. The Moon Goddess." Blackthorne's voice held a drop of frightful awe.

"Did you now, Mr. Blackthorne?" The edges of Captain Morrow's mouth quirked, a touch of arrogance creeping like groundwater into his smile. "Did she make an impression?"

Blackthorne smiled. "Maybe a little. She glowed all silver and pale blue, and walked on the moonbeams over the ocean tide. Her ashen hair wrapped around her shoulders like a cloak… and her sapphire robe sparkled like the stars. She was beautiful and fierce, and scared me to my bones."

The captain sighed, a memory gliding past his lips. "Aye. That was her." He glanced at the light over the horizon. "She may well be out tonight with the full moon and the storm. You could get another chance at a glimpse." He paused, not wanting to encourage his first mate's curious mood too much. "But don't try for more than a glimpse, or else she might take notice of you."

Captain Morrow heard the sharp intake of breath and knew his point had been made. The first mate's footsteps echoed away from him in a fading cadence, and the stern bark of his orders followed. Rafe smiled, a memory tickling at the edge of his mind.

The Navy of the Royal Court didn't know what they had, but I bless the fate that tossed Elliot Blackthorne to my deck. Not a more loyal man to be had in all the Seven Kingdoms or the Outer Islands.

Rafe felt the ship lurch under his feet as it leaned against the waves, deepening its eastern heading, and the sails furled out, billowed by the swelling wind. A stray finger of that wind ruffled the feather edges of Morrow's hair and skimmed the brim of his hat. A rich scent of orchid tickled his nose and a sense of magic tingled his skin, which set his blood pumping. Blue energy flickered off his fingertips, and in a heartbeat, his mood changed. He swivelled about, arms akimbo, and stared down his crew with a wicked grin.

"It'll be a wild night, boys, and a glorious one! Come what may, the sea's going to give us a ride this wondrous eve!"

The crew gaped in disbelief and bewilderment, but Rafe laughed. His eyes flashed a dark azure blue. "Ah, lads, we're not a bunch of lily-livered sops. I say bring on the Moon Goddess! Bring on her beasts of the sea! We'll send them back to the depths, every one!"

A cheer followed by laughter and guffaws rose from crew all around, accepting his challenge. With their blood fired up, their hearts raced the howl of the wind and the swell of the waves coming for them. Tonight, they would beat the storm to safe harbour, or face the consequences.

One-Eyed Anders hummed the notes of an old tune, and Captain Morrow tapped his foot in time. Short Davy started to sing:

Raise the sail, and say your prayers.
Come the moon.
Come the moon.
Come the sea-tossed moon

More voices joined in, and a lively noise threw itself to the dusky sky, a protection against the night.

Sail the storm
and say your prayers.
Come the moon.
Come the moon.
Come the sea-tossed moon.

Ward the magic.
Say your prayers.
Come the moon.
Come the moon.
Come the sea-tossed moon.

The monsters lurk.
so say your prayers.
Come the moon.
Come the moon.
Come the sea-tossed moon.

The ship echoed with the music, its structure taking heart and heed. The vessel heaved in the water, picking up speed, cutting a clip through the waves against the approaching gale. Standing at the stern, listening to his crew, the captain smiled.

"We make for Crickwell Island, men!" he shouted. "And damn the monsters!"

A cheer went up, its echo melding with the resounding notes of the song.

Come the moon.
Come the moon.
Come the sea-tossed moon.

Chapter Two
Crickwell Island

The ship made it two-thirds of the way to harbour before the storm hit. The blustering wind howled in first, rattling the sails and rigging like a loose pair of false teeth. Then the waves slapped the sides of the *Jewel,* pushing her against the sea and rebounding into her depths. The ship strained against the hands on her wheel, fighting the sea. One-Eyed Anders grunted, holding the wheel steady under the pressure until he felt a hand on his shoulder.

"I'll take the wheel. The storm's coming in too fast."

"Aye, Captain. We'll need our best man at the helm."

One-Eyed Anders relinquished the wheel to Captain Morrow and stepped off to other deck duties. Rafe felt the pull of the ship the moment his hands grasped the wheel.

"Come on, old girl. A little storm like this can't stop you."

A groan from the ship was her answer. She lurched against the sea, but the bucking of the helm eased within his hands. The sea tossed the *Jewel,* and she rolled from one side to the other but stayed upright.

The captain steered her low side into the oncoming storm and kept her steady, the increasing winds giving her speed, hopefully enough to outrun the edge of the tempest.

"Shorten the sail, boys!" Rafe said, tossing an order back to the crew.

"Already underway, Captain," came Pinky Jasper's reply, and Rafe smiled as he listened to the shouts on deck. He had a good crew. "Man the rigging, boys!" Pinky's harsh voice boomed, fighting to be heard over the wind. "If those square sails tear, there'll be hell to pay! Get the trysails up and keep 'em trim!"

As if his words were a spiteful prayer, the abrupt and frightful sound of ripping cloth reverberated down the mast and onto the deck. Rafe's heart skipped a beat and his white-knuckled hands gripped the ship's wheel. The ship lurched, and it was all he could do to hold her steady.

He heard more shouts and Blackthorne's voice, "It's the topgallant on the main mast! She's letting go! Get her down! Get her down! And bring down the main topsail! We don't want it going too!" The shouts were followed by a mad scramble of footsteps racing on deck.

Rafe glanced in their direction and saw the crew manning the lines. The tattered, damaged sheet and the remaining square-rigged sails came down faster than a drunken sailor's slur, while they hoisted the replacements in record time. Rafe breathed a sigh of relief for his ship before a wave slammed into the side and he yanked against the pull on the wheel.

"The sea's really starting to fight, lads! Keep your footing!"

Another vigorous wave stuck, and the sides heaved with a great moan. The great ship listed but sailed forward through the choppy seas. The ship rose on a sudden wave. Rafe tussled with the helm as the wave slammed down into the ocean. Salted spray, foam, and water washed across deck, and more than a few curses reverberated off the ship's bones.

More rolling and heaving as the ship raced onward under ever darkening skies, the waves growing larger and fiercer. Sea slopped over the deck and swept overboard assorted flotsam—loose tack, gear, and other bits left unsecured.

Abruptly, the ship lurched, the wheel slipping in Rafe's hands, and she heaved to the right, her hull at an angle. Rafe struggled to bring her to rights, barely holding her at a steady course among the crashing waves.

A haggard face burst out of the forecastle entryway from below deck. "A bloody gun hatch blew! We're taking on water!"

Rafe yelled, "Go, Blackthorne! See we don't sink!"

"Aye, Captain!" Blackthorne sprinted for the lower deck, shouting over his shoulder as he ran. "You have the main deck, Pinky! Keep those sails flying! Short Davy! Manfred! You're with me!" And with those words, Blackthorne and the other two crewmen disappeared below.

The whip-thin Pinky Jasper caught the order of the departed first mate and barked in return, "You heard him, crew! On alert! We'll ride this storm all the way to harbour!"

The crew echoed the cry. "All the way to harbour!"

The cheer rose to the charcoal sky as the clouds heaved and set free with rain that pelted the sea-tossed ship. Feet slid, curses bandied hither, and the crew turned to a wet drizzled lot as the ship cut through the roiling waves. The churning storm yowled with the guttural essence of a wounded sea beast. The turbulent wind thwacked the sails, its invisible fingers cuffing the cloth and tugging at its fibre.

As the wind caught the remaining sails, she sped her pace, battling against the storm. The salt-crusted liquid splashed on deck as the rain torrents cried down from the skies. Suddenly, that same sky ripped open, torn with the splinter of lightning and the boom of thunder. A streak of fear crashed over the crew.

"Gods save us! If that hits us, we're done for!" A wailing squeak piped out of a slip of a boy named Mouse.

"We only need one god, laddy," snapped One-Eyed Anders, "and he's at the helm!"

"Aye, he is!" Rafe grinned like a madman. "And by damnation, I'm master of this ship, and neither wind nor sea will sink her! It's time I show this storm what I can do!"

With his feet firmly planted on the surging wood of the deck, fingers holding a tight grip on the wheel, Rafe unleashed his power. His eyes glowed a pale blue, flecked with silver, and that same light poured from the wood and sheathed the circumference of the ship. The vessel shuddered, but not from the sea, or the elements, but from the primeval energy that emptied into its frame.

The light encompassing the ship shimmered and flashed, snaking down into the raging sea. As if in response, the sky roared with thunder. The murky clouds shook with wind and streaked with lightning. The waves reeled and swelled, but no angry sea waters reached the ship. Propelled on Rafe's magic, the grand *Celestial Jewel* sailed on to port, buoyed against the weather. Behind them, the wild storm still howled.

The ship sailed like falling starlight into the Crickwell Town harbour a short time later, having outraced the gale. Rafe steered her in to dock as a tired crew threw out the heaving lines and the shore workers pulled in the heavy mooring ropes. Working the capstans and by sight, both crews guided the damaged vessel into a berth without hindrance or trouble. Rafe gave a small sigh as they dropped anchors in welcome shelter.

Rafe slumped against the wheel, fatigue infusing his bones. He remained there, his breath, even. The sounds of his crew filled the night until a hand fell on his shoulder. He raised his head, and Blackthorne passed him a small glass full of amber liquid.

"Rum, sir. I thought you could use a drink."

The captain gratefully accepted the liquor and downed it in one gulp. The fiery rum burned into his gullet and its warmth infused his blood, taking the edge off his weariness.

He gave Blackthorne an appreciative smile. "I think I'll need a few more of those. But first I'll need to declare to the harbourmaster and give her fair warning of the storm. If she doesn't know already, that is."

Rafe handed the empty glass to his first mate, walked wearily across the deck, and disembarked, heading to the harbourmaster's office. Berthed ships crowded the harbour, but the docks stood strangely empty and quiet. No mooring crew in sight, no rowdy sailors, or even ruffians. Just the coarse wind scouring in from the sea. Rafe flipped up his collar and repressed a shiver. He quickened his step to the harbourmaster. Soon after affirming his ship's docking, he sat with a cup of hot tea in a tattered but comfortable chair across from an old friend, Ada Millar.

"Bit of a surprise visit from you, Captain. It's been an age since you wandered into Crickwell's port. Here for shore leave?"

"No. There's a wicked gale brewing out to sea. We barely made it to harbour ahead of it."

"What? There have been no reports. Is it headed this way?"

"Possibly. It shifted south as we came in, but it looks like it could be unpredictable. And it's a big one, so the edge of the storm should skirt the island in any case. You might want to batten things down as a precaution." Rafe finished his tea, knowing the woman would have duties to attend. "Sorry to bring unwelcome news."

"Better to have it before the storm hits than after. Most of our ships are docked already. Only the *Black Bastion* and the *Ocean Lily* are still headed in." A frown creased her face. "It's a moon cycle, too. Damn. I hope they're not caught out. Good men all aboard those ships."

For a moment, Rafe matched her worried look. "Aye. They're all good men." Then he replied softly, "Could be they turned back or headed to another port, first sight of the storm."

She nodded in agreement, not quite believing the words, but clinging to the hope. "Could be. No use fretting over trouble not come yet." She gave a slight nod and drained the last of her tea. "But, by the shoals, I hate the full moon and every last monster that comes with it." She let out a wistful sigh and gave Rafe a polite nod. "Thanks for the warning, I'll spread the word and prepare for bad weather." She rose to her feet. "I'm sorry our visit has to be so short."

Rafe smiled and stood. "Perhaps on our next trip, we'll have longer." They shook hands, and Rafe took his leave.

In the still air, his footsteps echoed as he walked, a discordant sound in the hushed night. He quickened his pace and felt relief as he returned aboard his ship. Rafe ran his fingers over the rigging and inhaled, savouring a hint of ozone and salt that drifted in the wind. Then he lowered his hand and walked towards the quarterdeck. Blackthorne met him at the bottom of the steps.

"Business squared away with the harbourmaster, Captain? How is she these days?"

"Yes. It's all taken care of, and she's quite well, by all appearances."

"Good. Then you've discharged your duty."

"Aye. Nothing more can be done there. How did the ship fair? Are we laid up, or is she seaworthy?"

"I have things in hand here, Captain, with the ship and repairs. No magic required, sir. But it will be a bad night tonight. I think our storm is coming inland. I can feel it in the air."

As if summoned, the wind swept across the deck. The sudden patter of rain echoed off the wood.

The Captain stared past the rail into the blustery darkness. "I think you're right. Looks like the weather's edge has hit the island. It'll be a wet night. The crew will be getting drenched this evening making repairs."

"Aye, but not too much. The damaged sail can be repaired as it just tore on the seam, and we've already replaced it from stores. I have men working on the rigging, as we'll need to splice a line or two. The mast suffered no damage. The gun hatch and things below are being attended to." Blackthorne paused in his speech with noticeable hesitation in his voice. Then he continued. "We'll be going back out then, after the storm?"

"Don't we always?" A bitter stain held in the words.

The first mate nodded, the faint moonlight exposing a sad tinge in his face. "I hope we don't find anything. I hope all the ships were in harbour tonight."

"So do I." The Captain sighed, a slight cheerless sound. "But two ships didn't make it into port here. They may have found shelter..." He broke off the rest and asked, "How long will those repairs take?"

A muscle in Blackthorne's jaw tightened. "An hour, maybe two or so. Not much overall. Mostly mopping of some puddles below deck. Lucky for us, the hull wasn't breached, just damaged port hinges and a latch. We mainly got tossed about. The galley looks a right jumble, though."

"Did we lose any provisions?"

"No. Things got knocked around, but no losses."

"Good. As soon as we're seaworthy and the storm breaks, we'll set sail again."

The wind blew across the deck, rattling loose odds and sods, and sending a chill down the Captain's spine. Rafe stared into the night and the roar of the heaving waves. His whisper followed the path of the storm.

"Please have found shelter. Don't be out there tonight."

Rafe sighed, and closed his eyes against the night, while somewhere across the world the eternal moon shone, and a Goddess sang a lullaby to her far-flung children.

The wishes and words scattered, pitched against the squall, but the sea and storm didn't heed. Far offshore in the wilding deep, a ship tossed on the rising, feral water, battling the screeching gales threatening to tear the vessel asunder.

The warrior figurehead glistened, dripping in the salt spray, the carved ship's name slick with foam. The silver lettering, *Black Bastion*, glittered in the shifting moonlight, echoing the challenge of the crew to the Moon Goddess.

We will not surrender! We will fight until the sea claims our last breath!

The crew believed in their name and the warrior upon their prow. A grizzled lot, toughened and weathered, they would not willingly yield a breath or a drop of blood to the stormy sea. Both ship and lives would need to be taken, clawed from the living and plucked from the cold ocean.

The *Black Bastion* plowed through the tempest, clashing against the elements. It soldiered on, creeping ever closer to shore. Luck and prayers held it together, with no certainty that fortune would stay with them.

Far to the southwesterly, in the full howl of the storm, another ship lost the fight. A cracked hull split full force, sails shredded, and the beast of the storm swallowed her whole. The ship and all hands were lost. Screams chased the *Ocean Lily* beneath the waves.

Chapter Three
Come the Monsters

As quick as the storm blew in, it blew out again, and the patched-up *Celestial Jewel* left the harbour at the first still wind. Captain Morrow strode across the deck, his confident step exposing none of his earlier trepidation.

"Full sail now boys, and all speed! We have a task ahead and the quicker we get to it, the better!"

A chorus of 'aye sir' echoed behind him as did the familiar tread of his first mate. "Did you see the *Bastion*, Mr. Blackthorne, as we left port?"

"Aye, sir. I did. In bad shape she was. Torn sail, busted masts, and a gash in her hull. Listing badly and most likely taking on water. She'll be laid up a while, but at least she made it in."

"With all hands, I hope?"

"I fear not. I heard she lost men. Not many, a few went overboard in the storm."

An imperceptible sigh escaped Rafe's lips. "What of the *Ocean Lily*? Any news?"

"No, sir. If there's anything to be found tonight, in all probability, it will be from her."

"And that's the question, isn't it? If anything's to be found. They'll be out tonight, and we'll have to be quick if we want to win the race. Look at the moon, Blackthorne."

The first mate glanced upward, staring at the rotund orb all glow and silver dazzling. It seemed to pulse in the sky, lighting the darkness like a beacon.

"It's as bright as I've seen and as deadly." Rafe's voice broke the spell. "She's in her element tonight. Her beasts will be roaming the seas. You can be certain of that."

"We're ready, sir. The weapons are primed and manned. We'll hold them off."

"If we get there in time, my friend. Only if we beat them to the wreckage." Rafe stared into the night, watching the ship cut through the waves. He turned his head back towards the crew and gave a shout, "Full speed and chase the moon, boys! We're in a race!"

His answer came with another chorus and the scurry of his men to obey.

⚓

As the *Celestial Jewel* sailed with all haste back into open waters, the seas spread calmer with a touch of undulating wildness, which reflected like black glass. The crisp air hit the crew with the force of a wench's slap. The smell of briny seaweed, fish, and death clung to it.

Captain Morrow sighed and tossed a command to the men at the rail on watch duty. "Keep a sharp eye on the waves. By all accounts and indications, there'll be salvage tonight." Answering hails echoed off the timbers, a sad agreement from the crew of what may come.

The ship veered west, and then to a more southern course, following the strains of moonlight, searching. The dark unfathomable waves slapped against the ship as the spotters leaned over the rail and peered across the depths. Radiance and chimera spun in their vision, nevertheless, their eyes faithfully scanned the ocean for life or death.

Suddenly, a smallish voice squeaked, "Something in the water!" Mouse raised a hand, pointing into the illuminated black. "Looks like debris!"

"The boy's right, sir!" The familiar baritone of Striker Angus shouted. "Wood to be sure, and white cloth! Could be a sail!"

"It don't mean a ship was lost!" One-Eyed Anders roared, voicing everyone's thought out loud. "Don't mean that. Could be they was caught, same as us. Just took some damage. Could even be from the *Bastion*."

"No." The Captain's soft answer washed over the crew. "We shouldn't speculate until we're certain. It's bad luck, that."

Still, the crew grew silent, no laughter, no banter, only their duties to man the ship and all available eyes on the sea. Despite clinging hope, the further out they sailed, the more shouts came as they spotted debris: fragments of wood and sailcloth, bits and bobs of individual possessions. The unmistakable flotsam of a shipwreck.

Then Rafe asked the question on the tip of every tongue, "Any sign of crew?" The indistinct silence gave him an unwelcome answer. "Perhaps—"

A screech broke past his words as if sensing the unease, a dreadful cry somewhere in the distance.

The shout of, 'Monsters' went up towards the sky. A brash gust of wind caught the sail, and the ship gained sudden momentum, cutting through the choppy waves. Spray bounced from its sides, and the crew bounded from their languor, spoiling for a fight. All hands made to man the ship's weapons, be it cannon, harpoon, sword, knife, billy club, or belaying pin.

With all nerves and tension slicing through the ship, Short Davy cried, "In the water! Hard about left! A floater with monsters coming up fast!"

The captain whirled, spyglass at the ready. Sure enough, the sea churned with the wake of beasts. "It's a pack of wolf eels, my lads! Get the harpoons primed, and ring that damnable bell! We've got a soul to rescue!"

The crew scrambled to ready the silver laced harpoons and their cannons, while Quiet Peter grabbed the bell pull and clanged with all his might. The magic fused into the metal surged across the ship and far out into the sea. Shivers cracked the air like an invisible whip, and every bone oscillated in the wake of the repeated peals of the bell. The poor wretch in the water convulsed and glowed, and the wolf eels screamed.

"Now lads! The harpoons!"

Sharp-tipped iron and silver sliced the air, and three harpoons landed true to their targets, smacking hard with the thud of metal in flesh and the swoosh of bloody spray. In one last screech to curse the dead, the beasts shattered, exploding into magic and meat. More eels swarmed, teeth gnashing, bubbling screams snaking through the water, as the desperate sailor thrashed and flailed in the sea.

Rafe yelled, "Another volley!" and more harpoons sang through the air slashing their targets. The ocean swirled in a bloody mess until the remainder of the pack retreated.

From the quarterdeck, standing proud and the wind blowing his coattails, Rafe shouted, "Come alongside, and cast the net before they try again!"

"Aye, Captain!" came the reply from Anders. The ship banked and manoeuvred parallel to the sailor. A net of star-woven rope was fired from the ship, another staunch aim. It scooped what lingered of the floating sailor and hauled him on board, the crank and tackle clanking noisily above the man's screams. Cast from the netting, dripping sea water, the fellow flopped about on deck like a prize fish.

"Are there any more?" Even above the wind, the captain's voice rang like a temple bell.

"No, Captain! That be it! Don't see another one in the water nowhere!"

"Full ahead then! Keep searching!"

As the ship sailed on, scouring the waters, Rafe turned his attention to their catch, bounding down to the main deck.

Soaked and terrified, the sailor scrambled on all fours like a crab, twirling around in circles "Get away! Get away!" The man's screams hit the deck like the dead weight of a drunken mariner. "I need to get away!"

"Take hold of yourself, sailor!" The voice of crew gunner, Striker Angus, snapped the night air, followed by the back of his hand against the man's cheek. "Ya ain't in the water no more!"

The shock of the blow and the words quieted his movement as he curled into a seated position, but did not silence his raving. "Not in the water? Are they gone? Please tell me they're gone. They were all around... all around... all fins and teeth. Swimming, swimming through the sea. I could hear them. Oh, by the gods, I could hear them! They were eating..." He shuddered and became quiet.

Rafe softly smiled belying the sadness in his eyes and spoke in a gentle, reassuring voice. "It's over, sailor. On this ship, you're safe from the monsters."

The rescued seafarer looked up, his body shaking. "I'm alive, then? I survived?"

"No, lad. I'm sorry. You're dead. You drowned. Went down with your ship. All that's left is your remnant, your spirit. That's what we pulled from the ocean."

The man twitched at the captain's blunt words, his head rocking back and forth. "No, no. You lie. I'm here. On a ship." He knocked his fist against the deck. "See, solid. Alive. I survived. I can't be... dead."

Rafe sighed. "Best you face it quick, sailor. Dead or alive, on this ship, it's all the same. You're dead, and your body will soon feed the sea creatures."

"No. No, no! I can't—I have to..." His words trailed off into a whisper as he stared into the quiet daunting face of Captain Morrow. "How can I be dead? I don't want to be dead."

"No one does. But at least we retrieved your soul from being eaten by the wolf eels. A fate far worse than death." Rafe extended his hand to the man who sat dribbling water on the deck, trembling, his mouth agape. "Welcome aboard the *Celestial Jewel*, a ship of sanctuary for the lost. I'm Captain Rafe Morrow, God of Souls."

Chapter Four
Coming Back

"What's your name, sailor?" Blackthorne's voice drifted calm and gentle in the salt touched air. He addressed the remnant who, newly fished from the sea, now huddled against the bulwark as the *Jewel* continued its grisly search. The task of comforting the rescued soul fell on his shoulders. He smiled at the pitiful scrap crouched in a shadowed crook on deck.

"I don't understand it. It doesn't make sense." The vestige of a man mumbled to himself, ignoring Blackthorne.

The first mate sighed and tried again. "I know it seems unfathomable with what's happened, but I can help. Let me help. Tell me your name, sailor."

For a moment the question went unanswered, but then the sailor looked at the first mate, his face awash in disbelief and misery.

"My name is Hugh Corwin."

"Hugh. A strong name that. I'm pleased to make your acquaintance Hugh Corwin even under these unfortunate circumstances." Blackthorne held out his hand.

Hugh shook the offered appendage gingerly. "How is this possible? If I'm dead, why didn't I cross to the After World? If I'm a spirit, how can I shake your hand?" Confusion tipped off his tongue and reflected in his eyes. "Wait. Are you dead as well?"

"No. I'm still alive. But some of the other crew are like you. Souls we fished from the sea's embrace. As to the how, this ship has a touch of the After World in her. She lets the ghostly dead stay as they were within her confines."

"Is that my fate then? To join the crew? To sail on some ship of doomed sailors? Never to cross, never to see my family again?"

Blackthorne heard the unshed tears and anguish in his words and put a comforting hand on his shoulder. "Where you go from here is your choice. As was the fate that left you bound to this mortal world."

"I don't understand. I—"

Sudden shouts interrupted.

"More debris to starboard, Captain! And looks like a sea wyrm coming in at full tilt!"

"Where there's one, there could be more. Man the weapons!"

At the interjected shouts, Blackthorne turned away from his charge with parting words. "This conversation will have to continue at a later date, Mr. Corwin. We've more trouble headed our way." The first mate sprinted off, leaving their newest ghostly resident open-mouthed and gaping across the unfolding scene.

An immense serpent rose from the ocean with the cry from the crew. "That's not a sea wyrm! It's a deep water basilisk!" Hugh stared, his body shaking. The snake-like beast stretched nearly as tall as the *Jewel*, with scaly, stubby wings and fins flapping in the wind. It spread its great maw and roared, spiky teeth glistening in the moonlight.

A flurry of harpoons and a series of cannon shots twanged and boomed through the night air, pelting the creature's hide in a barrage. The creature screeched and lashed the sea with its fearsome tail as wounds blossomed across its crusty skin. The *Jewel* bucked in the tidal wave, saltwater sloshing buckets over the deck. Sailors scrambled to grab hold of something and not be washed overboard. Hugh instinctively reached up and clutched at the ship's side, his arms wrapping tight around a cleat as the injured beast reared up for an attack.

"The beast is coming up! Ring the bell!"

The ship's bell clanged in a series of furious tolls, and the air crackled in the shivering magic. The beast's body rattled along skin and bone, and the creature screamed. A howl that gashed across air and sea stabbed past sensibilities and reason, piercing primal fear and provoking every instinct to flee. Hugh cried out, his voice ending on a whimper, but the crew didn't hesitate, launching another volley of assault. One harpoon punctured the creature's chest, and the creature fell back into the ocean, its body too grand to sink more than halfway into the water. Another great wave swamped the *Jewel*, pushing her around, and at the helm, Anders fought to hold her upright and steady. By the time she made it past the turbulent sea, the beast was gone.

"Any souls out there boys?" Hugh heard the captain's voice rise above the din, with the answering shout, "No sir! Either the beast got to them, or it was just trolling the waters!"

Hugh closed his eyes, shivering at the memories as Captain Morrow gave the next command. "Keep searching! If they're out there, we need to find them first!"

Hours later, Hugh still huddled in the shadowed corners of the *Jewel*, even though it rocked gently in the safe berth of the Abersythe port. The ship—after a night's search uncovered no more surviving souls, living or dead—had headed back inland, arriving in port well past dawn. The crew had retired for some much needed rest, leaving Hugh to his melancholy. Only now, as the sun crept low again on the horizon, did the deck stir again.

A shadow fell across the misery of the dead sailor. "I think it's time to finish our conversation."

Hugh looked up to see Elliot Blackthorne standing over him. "Why? What's done is done. I'm lost. No more choices. A dead man without a home."

"You have choices, sailor. You're not still in this world by caprice or the whim of the gods." Blackthorne snapped the words as if they were standing for inspection. "Something held you here tonight. Some thought or regret that prevented you from moving on to the After World. Find the answer to that question, and you'll be able to choose to cross or stay with us."

Hugh pursed his lips and furrowed his brows. "When the ship listed, when it went under, my last thoughts were of my wife." He glanced at Blackthorne. "We were only just married, not more than three months. I didn't want to leave her a widow."

"And it was enough to tie your soul here." A flash of regret bloomed and faded in Blackthorne's eyes. "You'll have to let her go to cross to the After World."

"Let her go? My Mary?" A sorrowful guise flashed across Hugh's face, half mourning, half dread.

Blackthorne gruffly exhaled. He hated the look they gave him. The same look every time. Different people, different families, but the same look. "I know it's a hard thought to consider, but—"

"And what if I don't want to let her go!" Hugh's

anger sparked up from his being, smacking the words against the night.

Blackthorne sighed. He hated the recalcitrant ones. "Then you'll be staying in this world. You can't cross into the After World still tied to this one." A stern expression slid over the first mate's face despite the gentleness of his next words. "There are places you can go until you decide. Until it all settles. We can find you residence at one of the island temples. Or we can give you a berth on the *Celestial Jewel.*"

Hugh scowled. "On this ship? Am I to be pressed into service then? Is that what this talk is about? Was I right? Another doomed soul on a cursed ship?"

A quiet exhale escaped the first mate. "No. None of that is true and you know it. Your fate from now on is your decision. However, if you stay here, you'll be in good company. Many a walking soul has remained as crew." Blackthorne paused, watching the anger and pain simmer under Hugh's glower. He considered ending the conversation but continued. "I must warn you though. If you do stay on, you'll not be able to leave the ship. Off its confines, you'll be naught but a shade haunting the living, unseen and unheard. Only here, or within the boundaries of a temple, can you be a semblance of what you once were."

The wretched look Hugh Corwin cast broke Blackthorne's heart as had every similar morose glare that came before. He hated this part of his duties.

Hugh stared at the deck. "So you're telling me all the stories I heard are true. It's happened. I'm not dreaming or still lost at sea. I died, and this is my end." Hugh glanced at the first mate, a look full of daggers and venom. "Here I sit, on board an unfamiliar ship, no wife or kin, surrounded by strangers. Nowhere else to go, save perhaps a temple with more strangers. Where's the choice in that? Where's the hope?"

"There's more hope here than what awaited you in the sea. Devoured, consumed and gone from this world and the next." Blackthorne's sympathy evaporated into a frown and a harsh tone. "On this ship, you still have the same hope as every soul: to pass on to the peace of the After World. Now you have to choose. You can sit and pout over your rotten fate or find a way to let go." Blackthorne straightened his spine. "I'll leave you to it then." He turned on his heel and left Hugh Corwin staring at his back. The echo of a name, Mary, ushered his departure.

The first mate crossed the deck to find the captain departing the ship. He quickened his pace and gave a shout. "Where are you off to, Captain?"

"A drink at the tavern. Care to join me?"

"I believe I would."

A glint of surprise crossed the captain's face, and then a smile. "Come then, Mr. Blackthorne, a long draught of ale awaits!"

The familiar sight of the salt encrusted, weathered wood of the Black Barnacle Tavern sent a spark of delight through Captain Morrow and even brought a smile to Blackthorne's lips.

"Almost like home, this place, eh Blackthorne."

"My home was a bit more civilized, but yes. It is a comfort after a night like the last."

The captain chuckled, and the pair walked into a noisy, half-crowded room full of sailors, labourers, and gamblers. The air smelled of ale and sweat, meat pies and sausage, and the hint of old fish. The sound of laughter, conversation, and the friendly clink of the glass enveloped them.

"There's a free table at the back, Captain, by the window." Blackthorne pointed through the crowd.

"So there is."

They wended through the boisterous gathering and slid onto worn wooden chairs that hugged a knife-scarred table. Captain Morrow flagged down a serving girl with a wave and a nod.

A familiar raven-haired tavern wench sidled to their table and flashed them a sweet smile. Blackthorne politely returned the smile, while the captain gave her a grin that guaranteed to flutter any heart.

With a slight giggle and a wink for Rafe, she asked, "What'll be for you two handsome gentlemen?"

"A dram of rum for me, Rachelle. And a beer for my first mate?" Blackthorne nodded.

"A beer and a rum coming right up, gents." Rachelle departed with a swish of her skirts and another wink for the captain.

"Captain Morrow! By the shoals!" A grating, gravelly voice intruded, falling upon Rafe and Blackthorne. A plump, grey-bearded man wearing a scar on his cheek and a woollen cap on his head ambled to their table. "It is you!" He slapped his hand on the table. "Do you remember me? Winston Jones."

Rafe flashed him a smile. "Winston! Of course, I remember you. Former scallywag off the *Nighthawk Trident*! How have you been, you old sea rat?"

"Can't complain for nothing, though I'm a land dweller these days. Retired, I am. Me and the missus run a fish market down harbourside." He chuckled. "I hear you've been up to your old tricks, though. Pulled one out of the jaws, I hear."

"Aye, Winston, we did. Barely got to him in time."

"For all the gratitude he showed." A soft grumble from Blackthorne caught Rafe's attention. He ignored it but tucked it away for later reference. Winston didn't seem to notice or didn't care.

"Glad you got to one at least. Right shame about the *Lily*. She was a fine ship and a good crew. Hope the rest went quick and didn't linger for food for them beasties."

Rafe held his tongue from the truth and, instead, tossed a lie to his friend. "No sign of that, Winston. With any luck, they passed over before the creatures arrived.”

“Good, good. Glad to hear it. 'Tis nice to see you again, Captain.”

“And you. Care to join us for a drink? I ordered some rum.”

Winston hesitated, as if contemplating, and licked his lips. But he shook his head. “Mighty kind of you, but I’d best get home to the missus. She’d have my hide if I’m late.”

“I understand. Farewell then.”

“Be seeing ya, Captain.” And with that Winston Jones turned up his collar and strode from the tavern.

Rafe leaned back in his chair. “So the word is out we have another soul on board. And one you don’t like, the poor wretch. He’s not taking his death well, Blackthorne?”

“Not well at all. More than per usual this one. A bit resentful, and angry. Sullen and spiteful. You think he’d rather have been eaten for all his self-pity. It never seems to change. They all take it hard, but this one...” A frown blossomed, then faded. “Last I saw of him, he’d found a corner of the deck to curl into, mumbling his wife’s name out loud.” A small sigh from Blackthorne’s lips hit the air. “Do you ever wish for something different? Than dealing with these souls? It’s hard what we do.”

Rafe’s smile turned wry and a bit bitter. A sad reflection looked back at his friend. “Neither one of us had much of a choice, now did we?” He idly traced a pattern on the table. “Not much point in wishing otherwise.”

"True, but sometimes I can't help but fancy the world wasn't so capricious, so harsh."

Rafe inhaled, and the air in the tavern crackled for a tiny frisson of a second. "Maybe you were born too late, my friend. The world was different once. Softer. Sweeter. The Goddess of the Moon protected the people. She was a good sister. My favourite sister." He softly sighed. "Back then sailors loved the full moon, for it meant a blessed passage across the sea." He paused briefly and then continued, his voice seeping regret. "But that was before she fell in love and went mad."

Blackthorne twitched. "Aye. 'Tis a sad story that. Maybe's that's my problem. Why dealing with those like Hugh bother me. Never loved enough that the loss would drive me mad."

The captain smiled, sympathetic and slightly amused. He couldn't imagine Blackthorne desperately in love. "Perhaps, but it may be a blessing. Love destroyed my sister as she destroyed her beloved, flesh and spirit." He traced a circle on the table with a finger, the memories bubbling up. "I warned her against it, her futile and misguided attempt to make him immortal." A small sound escaped his lips. Not a sigh. Not a wail. Something older, darker, and in-between. "She wanted me to fix it. To bring back his soul, but you can't restore or repair what no longer exists." A wry and sour grimace flashed through his lips quicker than a wave slapping the bow.

"But you've heard all this before."

"Aye, but I can listen again if you have the need."

Before Rafe could answer, Rachelle swished back with their drinks. "Here you go, a rum and beer." She clinked the glasses down with a smile and blew a kiss to them both as she left.

Rafe took a sip of rum, hoping to lighten his mood, but the feeling of morose sentimentality clung. The words tumbled out. "She hated me for that. For not saving him. It's why she embraced the madness so fully." He stared at his first mate, studying him for signs of languor or disregard, but saw only attentive commiseration. He idly wondered how many times he told this story after a full moon. He took another swallow of rum.

"She grieved so much, hated me so much, she birthed abominations onto this world, in the name of her wretched passion. That's the madness of love, Blackthorne." Captain Morrow turned his eyes to the window and stared at the harbour tide. "The horrors beneath our seas arose in defiance of her mistakes. The Kraken, the wolf eels, the black sea wyrms, and the other soul-eating ilk. Her dark, twisted spawn. Her children are her revenge on this world. Her way of punishing me."

He swigged the last of his rum and signalled Rachelle for another round.

Chapter Five
Ghosts

The next day dawned with a bright and cheery sunrise as if the previous storm and its lingering effects existed only in dreams and memories. Much of the crew came to duty nursing hangovers and sluggish with grumbles on their lips. Many took shore leave the night before to chase away bad memories, and the ale and grog flowed freely. This morning they paid the cost of their revelry.

Even Blackthorne felt the throb of an alcohol-induced headache, although it did nothing to stay his chastising of the crew. "Look lively boys, and keep to your duties! The salt air will do your wretched souls good!"

"Don't be too hard on the lads." Rafe stepped up on deck, chipper, and showing no signs of wear from the previous night's imbibing. "The lot of them are most likely feeling none too well." He grinned. "Especially you, Anders, I suspect. You fair drunk yourself under the table at the Black Barnacle."

One-Eyed Anders, despite his pale complexion and queasy expression, straightened his shoulders and retorted, "No sir, I can handle my liquor better than any man. Excepting you, of course, Captain."

"Good man. Carry on, the lot of you."

He strode past his men and beckoned Blackthorne into a private conversation. "Have you seen our newest sailor? Hugh, wasn't it? Hugh Corwin?"

"Aye, sir, but I haven't seen him this morning. I thought the surly wretch was brooding below deck."

"I searched. I wanted to have a chat with him, given what you told me, but no sign of him."

"Well, he isn't on deck, that much I'm sure of." Blackthorne frowned. "You don't think..."

"That he jumped ship last night? Aye, it's a possibility."

"Damn." Blackthorne's face flushed, his lips sporting an angry grimace. "Stupid fool. Bloody stupid fool."

His first mate's uncharacteristic profanity made Rafe twitch. "This one's truly gotten under your skin."

Blackthorne took a breath. "Maybe a little. He's going to be a handful. I knew it after speaking to him. Now we have an unsanctioned spirit running about town. If the harbourmaster finds out, we could face fines. Or worse."

"Don't worry about that. I'll go hunt him down. Everything will be well, Blackthorne."

Rafe gave him a grin and a reassuring clap on the shoulder before disembarking the ship.

The dockside appeared relatively lively in the morning sun, the busiest activity confined to the far wharves past his ship where two more vessels unloaded cargo. He wandered down, spotting no sign of Hugh and hearing nothing save the grunts and curses of the workers and sailors wrestling with the shipments.

Rafe moved inland to the marketplace above the docks. This place was quieter with only a few early traders setting up their wares. Without the usual crowds, searching the market proved simple, but gave no sign of the sailor so he moved on, winding his way along the cobblestone lanes back down to the docks east of the *Jewel*.

There, fifteen minutes later, he spotted Hugh.

The forlorn shade of the former sailor drifted beside those eastern docks, nothing more than a grey shadow invisible to all save him. Rafe moved alongside and in step with the ghost. Hugh said nothing, only shrugged a glance the captain's way. The pair moved side by side along the waterfront.

"How long did you try?" Rafe's voice finally broke the silence.

Hugh cast another glance in Rafe's direction. "Try?"

"To make yourself seen or heard. To rejoin the living."

"I—I didn't, I mean..." The lie trailed off, a hopeless bluff. "An hour, sir. I tried an hour. Shouting, cursing, begging. None of it to any use. I don't exist anymore. Not here among regular folk. I'm just a remnant. A sad scrap without the sense to die properly." He tried to kick at a loose stone. His foot passed through the rock.

Rafe sighed, a sad acquiescence to fate. "Sometimes I wonder if any of us has sense, young man, to live or *die* properly."

Hugh shot him a baffled look, and Rafe smiled.

"We can only do what we do, and make the best of the consequences. Come back to the ship, and we'll talk."

Hugh stopped moving, standing as still as the doldrums. "Why, sir? Is there a point?" Bitterness dripped faster than overflowing ale. "Talking won't fix anything. I'm—I'm—well, you know, and there's no going back. You should have left me to the sea. Better nothing than this half-existence."

"Well, aren't you full to the brim with self-pity." Rafe matched Hugh's bitter attitude with his own disdain. "I've seen souls consumed by her beasts, and I wouldn't wish that fate on the worst of my enemies." Something akin to a shudder pulsed through the captain. "So no, being left in the sea is *not* preferable. And you won't be abandoned to wander about, either. You will report back to the ship, sailor. For a good dressing down if need be. That's an order!"

Hugh snapped to attention by habit, with a smart, "Yes, sir!"

Rafe chuckled softly. "Or, we could just have a talk. Your choice, Mr. Corwin."

Hugh's ethereal form relaxed. "A talk, sir, I suppose."

"Good lad. Back to the ship then shall we?" Rafe

motioned with his hand.

Hugh nodded and the pair slowly ambled the length of the Abersythe docks to the *Celestial Jewel.*

"I didn't believe you." Hugh's voice barely lifted, but Rafe heard the resignation in his words. The emotional resonance bounced around the captain's quarters as Rafe watched him pace the room.

"I know. Very few souls do in the beginning." Rafe said the words in a calm voice, although his patience slipped near the edge. He spent the last half hour dealing with Hugh's unconstrained wallowing, but it seemed as if the boy was finally winding into acceptance.

"You hear stories, you know. About your ship. About what you do. But I never supposed they were true, not all of it. Every sailor knows your ship, but ghosts and the like, it didn't seem real. A tall yarn spun to pass the time."

Rafe smiled. He had heard the stories too, some accurate, some outlandish lies.

"I guess I didn't want to believe. Or thought I didn't need to. No sailor likes to dwell on dying."

"Very few souls, sea or land, like to think on dying. Not until it happens. Then a soul has no choice." Rafe's voice was kind but firm. "Now you have to consider it. You have to acknowledge your existence and decide on its fate. On whether to stay or go. And whichever you choose, know your former life is over."

"That's the trouble. It doesn't feel over." Hugh's voice sang in desperation and ache. "All I want to do is go home. Hold my wife in my arms and see her smile." He sighed. "But that's never going to happen again, is it?"

"No. Death, in whatever form, is a finality."

"But if I could just see her, try and say goodbye..." He turned to Rafe. "If you could help, maybe we... we could..." The words slid out to sea as Rafe glared.

"It doesn't work like that. For her, life will move on. If you try and remain with her, you will prolong the heartbreak." Rafe's voice softened, his tone trying to soothe the harsh certainty. "Your ship was reported lost. She will be mourning your death, Hugh. Let her mourn in peace."

A shiver quaked through Hugh's ghostly form. "I—I didn't think—she knows I'm dead?"

Rafe nodded. "If she doesn't, she will soon. As will your family. All notifications about lost ships went out hours ago."

"Oh, poor Mary." Hugh flopped down in a chair. "Then it's—it's done. I'm dead. I'm truly dead to everyone I knew." He looked at Rafe, a thousand cares written in his eyes. "What am I to do? I don't feel dead. I feel—feel the same as I always have. I still feel... alive, I suppose. How can I pass on like that?"

"It may take time. The heart doesn't always let go of

life easily. Some never do." Rafe smiled. "But I believe you will be one to go on to the After World. Just stay on the ship. Give it time."

"Time. I suppose that's all I have left." Hugh exhaled, a small grey mist stirring in the air. Then blurted, "What is it like, the After World?"

A strange, far-off look glazed against Rafe's eyes. "It's beautiful perfection. All emerald green and shades of blue with silver and amber light. The air smells of flowered perfume and salty brushed sea, the temperature is warm and a balmy breeze blows just enough. Everyone has a smile, and a laugh, and never a cross word. It's all the comfort and peace a soul can want."

Hugh sighed, a quick breath of longing. "It does sound like a lovely place." And in a quiet whisper, "Almost too lovely to exist."

Rafe ignored the comment, still reminiscing, "Aye, it was. And still is, I suppose. For a time it was my heart and home."

"Was your home?" Hugh shot Rafe a surprised look. "Do you mean—You used to live there?"

"Aye, lad. I did. A long time ago."

"Why did you leave?" Sudden vibrant curiosity scurried into Hugh's face. "Do you miss it? You made it sound a paradise. Why would you leave such a wondrous place?"

"I left for good reason, and no, I don't miss it. The sea is my home now. From the salt to the dark depths, from the monsters to the moon. And a far better one, than the place I came into being."

Hugh frowned. "I don't understand. How can you say that I'll find peace, but then swear you're happier here? That doesn't make sense."

"Gods and mortals have a different perspective, young man. Your kind enters into paradise. Mine… well, we're a prickly sort, not prone to getting along. The place may be a paradise, but my kind is not." He shot Hugh a wry smile. "But don't you worry, humans don't have dealings with them in the After World."

"Is that why you left? Family squabbles?"

Rafe hesitated, considered not answering, but in the end replied, "I didn't leave. I was cast out. Turned into a fallen deity. So, you see, my memories of the After World are tainted, I'm afraid." Then Rafe grinned, trying to make light of his words.

But Hugh's frown persisted. "A paradise you said, yet... What if I decide not to go? Stay on this side forever?" Hugh's questions spun out of gossamer threads, the monster lurking under the surface.

Rafe shrugged. "Then you stay here. In the form you are, ghost to all save those on this ship, or in the temples. That's your choice, Hugh, if you remain. Wander the land unseen, reside in a sanctuary, or join the crew of the *Jewel*." Rafe tilted his head, studying Hugh's expression. "Why would you be considering staying? I understand for a while, to sort things out, but why a permanent stay?"

Hugh remained silent for a moment, and then he sputtered, "I'm fearful." His whisper barely rose above the sound of their breathing, but Rafe heard it.

"Why? What frightens you?"

Hugh cast his eyes downward. "Of being forgotten. Of being alone. What if no one remembers me? What if no one is waiting to greet me in the After World? I've had family that have passed, but why would they know me now? It's been years."

"Is that all?" Rafe clucked his tongue like a fisher's wife. "Because the world beyond doesn't work like that. Family is drawn to new arrivals. There will be someone there."

Hugh raised his eyes, a shimmer of unshed tears lacing the rims. "But she won't be."

"Your wife?"

He nodded. "You said it. I'm dead to her. She'll move on without me. It won't matter if I wait for her. She won't be waiting for me. She'll have the life I've been denied. With someone else. We'll never be together again."

Rafe sighed. The young man saw too much for his own good, and not enough. "Things are more complicated than that, Hugh. Infinitely so in the After World. If you're in her heart, she'll remember you. You'll see her again. Perhaps not as you once were, but you will see her."

"It just isn't fair. We should've had time. We should've had a life together."

"That you should. And I have no true answer to your dilemma. Life doesn't play fair, Hugh. Good men die sometimes. Good women are widowed. And everything continues. Whether there's a pattern or a plan, I cannot say. I've never seen one. I just gather the scattered pieces."

"Like me."

"Like you."

Hugh grumbled, "That's what a life comes to then, a bit of sea salvage, jetsam?"

"Better than being eaten out of existence," Rafe snapped back, letting his irritation show. Then he sighed. "It's obvious you are still raw. Go back on deck. Get some fresh air. Think about what I've said."

"Is that an order, sir?" Hugh sneered slightly to accompany the words.

Rafe's patience finally cracked. "Would you prefer a boot up the backside?" Rafe took momentary satisfaction in Hugh's shocked expression. "And yes, that's an order. Get out of my sight before I do something I'll regret."

Hugh stood, head lowered, and left without another word, wandering back to the deck as ordered. He went to the rail and placed his hands on the recognizable surface. He could feel the rough wood of the rail under his fingers and hear the splash of the harbour tide as it caressed the ship. It seemed palpable. He felt alive no matter what anyone told him.

Yet, it wasn't.

"It's only an illusion. Only good aboard ship." This small murmur of misery lifted on the breeze. Hugh sighed.

"Coin for your thought, and silver for the moon." A small voice broke through his melancholy and Hugh whirled about in surprise. At the action, the speaker yelped and a frightened face ducked behind a raised arm.

Immediately contrite, Hugh spit out, "I'm sorry. You just startled me."

The arm lowered and the timid face of Mouse peeped out, and then smiled. "Guess I'm the one who should be sorry then for spooking you first." Mouse sidled in next to Hugh, leaning on the rail. "I came to say hello, you looked a bit sad."

"Shouldn't I be? Trapped on a strange ship, my berth gone to the bottom of the sea. Can't say that makes a man cheery."

"Wouldn't think so. It's not an easy thing dying. But it could be worse, you could be food for the monsters." Mouse shivered. "Or lost in the world."

"Would that be worse? Not existing or trying to reconnect? I'm not sure."

Mouse shook his head, a squeak of protest darting into the morning air. "Then you're daft. I know it's hard, but I can't imagine wanting to be monster chow instead." The lad put a hand on Hugh's arm. "Let it happen. It feels like you're cooped up on the ship at first. It gets better, it does. Once you get used to things, you can go ashore with the crew. The ship's magic, you see, seeps into the blood of the living crew that stays on board the *Jewel* for any length of time. They become able to see us spirits when they are off the ship." Mouse smiled and then gave a faint sigh. "It's a good life, and trust me, wandering out there alone is an awful thing." Mouse waved his hand at the lively port. "Being invisible, them regular folk not seeing you, hearing you." The boy shuddered. "I know. I was lost for a long time before the captain found me."

Hugh started, the realization dawning this lad was like him. A shade, a ghost.

The boy smiled. "Yeah, we're the same. I know how you feel. And you'll find your way, whether you stay or cross over."

A fleeting wry smile passed over Hugh's face. "That's the question, isn't it? Staying or leaving to the next world." He brushed a thumb over the wooden rail. "Why did you stay here?"

Mouse blushed and scuffed his toe on the deck boards. "It may seem silly, but the crew's my family. I ain't never had one before. Not a proper one. Just me Da." Mouse shivered, his hands tightening into fists. "He was bad, me Da. I'm afraid to cross. Afraid he'll be there waiting. Captain says he won't be, that men like him go somewhere else, but..." His face twisted to a mask of melancholy awash with a nightmare.

Hugh reached out instinctively and placed a hand on Mouse's shoulder. For a moment, surprise jolted him. The contact felt solid like the flesh they once possessed. Then he remembered. On this ship the rules were different.

"How did you die?" The words came from Hugh's mouth before he thought. Regret came swiftly after, but Mouse didn't seem to mind.

"I was a cabin boy on board the *Sapphire Isle*."

Hugh blinked with a sharp intake of breath. It couldn't be. Not that famous old wreck.

"I see you've heard of it." Mouse grinned. "And yes, I've been here a while. Didn't get salvaged though after death. My soul got swept in an undertow and back to land eventually. I barely saw the beasties. Captain said they took a lot of sailors that day." Mouse sighed, and then ventured a question, "Do you remember the monsters?"

Hugh nodded. "Dark, dreadful shapes in the water. It's the sounds I remember most, though. The howl of the wind and the screams. The horrid screams. They were my friends, my crewmates, but in the end, I couldn't recognize the voices. I heard them die, and I didn't know who."

Mouse looked out over the port. "I'm glad I don't remember that. I remember these horrible yowls and the darkness of the sea. And the fear. Then finding myself on shore. I thought I was safe. I was alive. Silly of me, right?"

Hugh closed his eyes for a moment. "No. Not silly at all."

"Sometimes I wish the ship had found me that day."

Mouse turned his head and stared at Hugh, making him shiver with the intensity of the gaze. "Have you been surrounded by people, but still alone? Screaming to be heard, day after day, year after year? You come close to madness, you do. So alone that you want to die. Except you're already dead." He turned his face away. "The ship's a better fate than that. Trust me."

Hugh joined Mouse in the quiet contemplation of Abersythe harbour, his memories of his frustrating morning melding with the sinking of his ship. He began to consider that he may not have been as unlucky as he thought. That the *Celestial Jewel* might, after all, offer hope.

Chapter Six
Attacked

"That's it! Get that final crate loaded, and don't forget that last keg of ale!" From the dock, Rafe shouted to the deckhand with a smile as he oversaw the loading of provisions and supplies aboard his ship. He spied Hugh and Mouse helping out on deck, and a glimmer of optimism for the new soul flickered.

At least he's trying to fit in. That's a start.

"Captain Morrow!" A hail broke off his musings, and Rafe turned to see the harbourmaster rushing towards him.

"Captain, a word if you please! It's an urgent matter." The short, slim gentleman darted with considerable swiftness dockside before halting beside Rafe. "Thank goodness I caught you still in the harbour." Panting slightly, he craned his neck to look the captain eye to eye.

Rafe frowned. "Is there a problem? I know I've paid the harbour fees."

"Oh, yes, indeed there's a problem! A calamity, I'm afraid! I've received a dreadful missive from Llansfoot and the Temple of Star Reef!" A pained sigh escaped him. "They've sent word by spellcaster. There's been an attack on the port and the temple!"

A chill infused Rafe's blood. Only the worst news came by spellcaster. And if it involved the Temple... "An attack?" He barked the words out on a wave of his apprehension. "Tell me, what misfortune's befallen Llansfoot?"

"Monsters." The word split the foundation of the air between them. "The seas attacked in force at dawn. Creatures rising from depths to assail town and temple."

"What? That's impossible!" Shock jolted Rafe's nerves as if lightning had struck him. "They can't! They just can't! Her beasts shouldn't be able to stir without the turn of the moon let alone attack a town! No monster should be able... She's bound by... Are you certain?" Rafe abruptly grasped at the hope of a mistake.

The harbourmaster nodded. "The message was clear. The beasts of the deep attacked in force."

Rafe repressed a shiver. "Even if they rose without moon or storm, they search for shipwrecked souls. They've never harassed a settlement. It makes no sense. They only go after the dead." Unexpected fear struck him as a hull on hidden shoals. "The temple. They went after the temple. To feed on all the souls waiting to cross."

"Yes, Captain. I believe so. This is why I relayed the

news to you with haste. It appears the rules have changed, my friend. From what I gathered, the worst assault came to those on Star Reef." Another sigh preceded his next words. "You must sail to Llansfoot. They need you. They need their God of Souls."

For an instant, in the turn of time, Rafe wanted to refuse: to climb aboard his ship and sail to the furthest point he could find. Something in his bone and blood shouted that this moment would be a turning, a watershed, and he ached to flee.

Yet, he never ran from a fight, nor the truth. Not once in all his long years.

So instead he replied, "I'll set sail for the port as soon as we're able."

The harbourmaster exhaled a final sigh and shook his hand. "Fair wind, Captain, and the best of luck. I fear you will need all that may be spared."

⌂

A few hours sailing put them in the vicinity of Llansfoot well past the midday sun, with truth and rumours sounding off the ship in a reverberating maelstrom. A mood of apprehension turned the crew into a jumpy lot full of frayed nerves and silence. Even Blackthorne seemed more taciturn and rigid than his usual want of disposition. And the captain, well... Grim only touched the edge of his disposition.

"Around the reef and we'll see the Temple!" Rafe gave the shout and heard it echo into stillness, riding a frisson of disquiet that undulated across the crew. He turned his head, watching them at work.

They're scared. Not that I blame them. The world's not right here.

Rafe sighed deeply with worry. The temple at Star Reef was his shining star, the largest of the sanctuaries dedicated to his name. Hundreds of souls awaited there, attempting to resolve their issues and pass through to the After World.

How could she send them there? It isn't possible. There are rules. Bindings. It must be a mistake. Yet... something's wrong. Something's shifted.

As much as he wanted to deny the impossible, he could sense a surfacing upheaval deep in the ancient marrow of his being. The closer they sailed, the more unease settled. With an imperceptible shudder, he turned back to stare at the sea as the *Jewel* rounded the last bend and the reef.

"By the depths! Look!"

The shout shattered the unnatural calm, but no one needed the goading. Moans and gasps rose on the wind as all eyes stared towards the shore. Where once outlying buildings stood, only wisps of dawdling smoke greeted them, ascending from charred remains and blackened earth strewn with broken shapes. Great chunks of stone, pieces of the shattered seawall, jumbled across the beach leaving huge gaps in the wall. Shadows and movement slid over the sand, and faint, heart-wrenching cries could be heard, conjuring despair as they softly mingled with the sea breeze. And as they sailed, further destruction came into view.

"What happened?" Rafe heard the whisper of Hugh drift over his shoulder. "I thought the temples were a sanctuary. A safe haven."

"No longer, I fear. No longer." The ache in Rafe's heart bubbled past all defence as he answered, and his unstoppable wail broke the air. Behind him, he heard the crew's shocked reaction, but he didn't care. Only sorrow and pain mattered as he viewed the ghastly sight of the Temple of Star Reef… what remained of it at any rate.

Rafe stared, remembering the majestic white marble twin towers and the beautiful enclosure of the main edifice. In his mind's eye, he saw the colours of the blooming garden and smelled the fragrance of its flowers and fruit trees. He wanted to close his eyes and lose himself in the memory, deny the truth before him on the shore, anything but seeing the condition of it now.

"Why, sister? Why?"

The words didn't erase the sight, nor did his wishing. The crumbling ruins of the right tower scattered across the land and the shallows, leaving a gaping hole shattered into the temple proper. The ornate, carved wooden entry gates swung half-broken on twisted hinges, revealing the devastated front gardens. Smashed hedges, battered and broken trees and long gouges sliced into the earth were all that remained of its beauty.

Rafe drew in a painful breath. To see one of his places, one of his sanctuaries that stood refuge for lost souls so damaged...

Caught among the rubble and splintered foliage, fragments of stone and roof tile could be seen strewn about, dispersed without pattern or care. And on the remnants of the temple still standing, hung hollows and breaks that crisscrossed the vestige of the structure.

What has become of you?

While the visible damage wrenched at his soul, Rafe saw past the physical. He saw the living and the dead milling aimlessly, some wailing, some silent. Long-standing ghostly residents hovered with the freshly departed, men and women he knew in life. Priests most likely killed in the carnage.

"The temple wharf seems intact. Should we pull ashore here, Captain?" Blackthorne's voice tugged him back. Lost in his desolation, he never heard him approach.

"Yes, Mr. Blackthorne." Misery couldn't hold itself from his tone, but he gave the command. "We'll put ashore here first. I have to talk to the Grand Master. But don't settle in, we'll most like be moving further along the shore to Llansfoot."

"Do you want us to dock or anchor offshore?"

"We'll dock. I'll take her in myself. There'll be no shore crew to help us this time. The *Jewel* will have to guide herself."

Blackthorne gave the orders to the crew, and the captain took the helm, Anders stepping away with a knowing nod. Rafe placed his hands on the wheel, brushing his fingers over the wood with reverence. Blue light emanated from his fingertips and twirled around the wheel, sliding into the grain and wending its way into the mechanics of the ship. Soft whispered words slid over his tongue. "Wake up. It's time to come into harbour."

For a moment, nothing, and then a wave of sapphire sparkles danced across the deck before spinning upward and setting the sails alight in momentary radiance. Rafe manoeuvred the wheel, letting the feel of ship guide him inland. Then he released his grip on the wheel and took a step back.

"All right, old girl. Take us in."

The ship creaked and heaved, and the helm adjusted course with no hand to steer it. Sails trimmed themselves, and the speed slowed, the ship gliding effortless across the sea to the temple wharf. Without a hitch or misstep, the vessel dropped anchor and docked itself in the Star Reef harbour.

As the ship settled in its anchorage, the captain strode off the quarterdeck. "Time to go see to the troubles, men."

A small contingent of crew accompanied Blackthorne and Rafe ashore. As they navigated the ruins, they soon realized stone was not the only thing broken and decimated. Bodies of the priests and others still scattered the wreckage as well. The shapes they spotted on shore as they sailed in.

"Why? By all that's holy, why here?" A wail from Pinky pierced the air. "What did this?"

A sigh from Anders answered him. "Nothing good, nothing good."

Rafe listened, looked at the horror, and his fingers curled into fists. "No, gentlemen, nothing good at all." Movement caught his attention, and he saw a priest walking towards them.

"Welcome sirs, even in this time of trouble. How can—" The priest stopped in mid-sentence, recognizing Rafe. As the captain approached him, the priest fell to his knees in veneration.

"Forgive us. Forgive us, Exalted One, for not protecting this holy place." His body trembled and his anguish lashed the circling wind.

Rafe sighed, another corner of his heart snapping. He knelt down and placed a comforting hand on the man's shoulder. "You need no forgiveness. I'm here to help. What happened?"

The priest stammered incoherently and genuflected as unsure and as gangly as a beached sea creature. For a moment, Rafe thought he might kiss his boots.

"No need for that. Please, rise." Rafe reached down and helped the man to his feet. The priest stood but kept his head lowered, refusing to look Rafe in the eyes.

"Is Kyyn here? Did he survive?"

"Yes, Exalted One. The Grand Master still lives." The words spilled like loose salt, hushed and tiny. "He tends to the injured in the hall. It stands undamaged."

Rafe breathed out a small sigh. "Thank you. You may go now." The priest scurried away in a crab-like manner, head downward backing off. Rafe watched him retreat before addressing his men.

"I'm going to talk to the Grand Master, see the extent of what happened here. Make yourselves useful and help with whatever these people need." Without waiting for an answer, Rafe stalked off, certain his crew would follow orders.

He crossed through debris and ruin, seeing score marks in the tower rubble as he passed as if raked by claws. He climbed over a breach in a fractured garden wall and turned past the corner of the outer temple towards the inner sanctuaries. Here, the damage seemed minimal, and, as he approached the communal hall, it appeared entirely untouched.

He entered through the open door unnoticed. A cheerless, low chorus of pain moaned to him as he surveyed the pallets and beds holding the injured. Priests and settlers both filled the space either as patient or caregiver, and the air stank of blood, sweat, and horror. He spied his friend, Kyyn, Grand Master of the Temple of Star Reef, sitting by a bed bandaging the arm of an injured woman.

He looked up as Rafe approached. The captain gave him a sigh and a greeting. "I'm glad you're well, old friend. Despite the devastation I see around us."

"And I am glad to see you, Exalted One. We are in need of your guidance and aid." The Grand Master finished his bandaging task, before leaving his patient in the care of another healer. He joined Rafe and beckoned him to a walk.

"What happened to the temple, Kyyn? Was it truly attacked by her monsters of the sea?"

The Grand Master turned his head staring for a moment at the destruction. "It doesn't seem possible, does it? Her children are forbidden, restricted by the magic geas you placed on them. Yet, it happened. A pack of black sea wyrms attacked at sunset with no warning." Rafe saw a delicate shiver chase along the priest's skin. "I had never seen them before. Few who stay ashore have. Such beasts, they were, the awful roaring, people screaming, panic and chaos." He shook his head in sorrow and remembrance. "And not only here, but in the town as well, although the brunt of their attack…" A look of regret passed over his face. "They came to destroy.

Such horrid violence. Smashing against the Temple with their slashing tails, skittering from the sea across the beach, their ravenous jaws causing so much death." Kyyn paused, a film of tears at the edge of his eyes, and a catch in his breath. "If it only ended there. The worst of it—the worst thing—" A quiet sob broke through. "You must know, you must know what they did!"

"They consumed the waiting souls, didn't they?" Rafe's voice was faint and held the mourning of a thousand horrors.

The Grand Master nodded. "Yes. Near half of the unfortunate remnants still remaining. Vanished. Gone from life, death, existence. Consumed. Some were so close, and now..." Kyyn sighed. "At not only the waiting ones. My priests and those of the outlying settlement: poor souls newly killed by the creatures without a chance to cross. And more, by all accounts, in Llansfoot."

Rafe closed his eyes and halted his steps. The pain stabbed at him, gnawing a new hole in his already tattered heart. A desperate question formed on his lips, forestalled by Kyyn.

"No, I do not think this was a random madness of her beasts. Or an aberration."

Rafe's eyes fluttered open again. "You know me too well, Kyyn. You think the Moon Goddess had her hand in this?"

"I do. She sent them here. She's broken the binding and coming for you. The attacks were too coordinated, too precise, too planned. She directed her creatures to this violence." He sighed. "She struck at you, Exalted One, using your temple as a surrogate. I do not know why or how, but she is the one behind this. Of that I am certain."

Rafe turned away, looking out to sea. He whispered, "What do I do?" his words floating as a poignant entreaty on the wind.

Kyyn patted his shoulder. "What you must to safeguard the world, Exalted One, as must I. But for now, we pick up the pieces from these ruins." He took a breath and exhaled. "Come I will show you and your men where best to help." He laid a hand on Rafe's arm. "It is help we welcome. The Temple ranks are greatly diminished by this attack."

The Grand Master strode into the wreckage. Rafe followed him. Soon, he and his crew were helping the priests collect and bury their dead, and look after those left alive.

From the temple, they sailed on the small distance to Llansfoot, the sun shifting towards the horizon. The town fared much better than the Temple, its seawall being a sturdy, thicker construction. But even so, many shanties, fishing shacks, boats and ships lay in shattered parts as well as several docks, and some of the port. They spied groups of people working to slowly clear away rubble and damaged boats.

"The harbour is filled with debris, captain. Going to a berth will be tricky. It might be best to anchor offshore a bit, and travel by longboat." As usual, Blackthorne was quick with his advice.

"I agree. Find a spot, set the anchors, and prepare a landing party."

"Aye, Captain." Blackthorne set to work and soon, a party of five crew plus the captain and the first mate navigated the wreckage and came ashore on the Llansfoot beach, east of the port. A group of fisherman salvaging some of their tackle eyed them suspiciously.

One gave a shout, "Hey to you! What's your business here?"

Rafe answered. "'Tis Captain Morrow and crew come to offer aid to Llansfoot."

A hiss and a gasp echoed across the sand and rock, and the men doffed their caps in hasty respect. "Oh, Captain, apologies. You'll be wanting the Lord Mayor and the harbourmaster. They're up at the port proper seeing to the damage and the cleanup. Take the beach path in. 'Tis clear."

With a nod and heartfelt thanks, the men beached their boat above the tide mark and headed up to the port. Rafe glanced back and, for a brief moment, watched the fishermen scrounge through the wreckage.

"I wonder what they lost? Livelihoods? Loved ones? Both?"

None of his crew answered, and they trudged the rest of the journey in silence.

As they hiked into the usually bustling port, only the sounds and sights of the calamity's aftermath were apparent. At the water's edge, men repaired boats and ships or hauled away splintered wood and broken stone. Others gathered washed up debris and gear or brought food and drink to working men. And tucked away, past a still intact dock and jetty, lay two small rows of dead men covered in white shrouds.

"Why are the bodies still out in the open like that? 'Tis disrespectful." A harsh whisper drifted from Pinky.

In an equally low voice, Rafe tossed an answer back. "I'd wager they recently washed up and were fished out. They'll haul them away soon enough."

Pinky ducked his head at the soft rebuke, and they trudged the rest of the way to the harbourmaster in silence. A tired-eyed and haggard-faced Lord Mayor scurried over and greeted them as they arrived.

"Captain Morrow." Equal parts relief and fear mingled in his voice. "Gentlemen." He gave a nod to them all. "You are most welcome, though I wish it under better circumstances that you come. As you can see, it's been a long hard night, and morning."

"Yes. Both the port and the temple have suffered greatly."

"You've been to the temple? Then I suspect you'll be wanting our account of the attack." Rafe nodded. "Come,

come, best be discussed inside." He took a step towards the harbourmaster's door, but Rafe laid a hand on his shoulder.

"A moment. My crew is not needed for explanations. They can help with your troubles while we talk."

"An excellent suggestion. They can report to the harbourmaster, down at the Breakwater Dock. Are you familiar with it?"

"Aye, we know it." Rafe turned to his men. "Blackthorne, take the boys down and lend a hand while I chat with the Lord Mayor."

The group separated, and the captain and his companion retired inside the shelter of the harbourmaster building. They settled into two worn chairs, and the Lord Mayor poured some whiskey found on a shelf into chipped mugs. He handed one to Rafe.

"Here, Captain. I think we both could use it."

Rafe accepted and took a sip, then asked, "Grand Master Kyyn said they were attacked by black sea wyrms. Was it the same here?"

"Yes, a swarm of them attacked the sea wall and did some damage as you no doubt saw coming in. But the wall held. It was on the fishing boats outside the port, and those sailing home, they wreaked the most horror. So many lost." The Lord Mayor bowed his head in a moment of remembrance before continuing. "They retreated when the crew of the *Whistling Teacup* turned her guns of the beasts and drove them back, brave lads. We were lucky the ship was just coming into port, and not yet docked, or we might have fared worse. Especially with what happened next."

"There was more? The sea wyrm came back for a second attack? That's not like them."

"Not the sea wyrm. A blood fin titan. It did the most damage in the port with its tentacles and pincers. By then though, we had the port's cannon primed, and we finally drove it back as well."

"A blood fin titan?" Rafe couldn't keep the incredulity and dread out of his voice, though he tried. "Are you sure?"

"Aye. And I know. One of them hasn't been sighted close to shore in nigh on a hundred years. Can't say I was happy to have the privilege." The Lord Mayor gulped his whiskey and turned a worried face to Rafe. "Tell me, Captain Morrow, is she coming for us at last?"

Startled by the question, Rafe blurted "I don't know."

The Lord Mayor sighed. "I was afraid of that. I bloody hope you can find out before we all die."

Rafe stared a moment into the whiskey, before downing the remainder, and giving an answer. "I'll do my best, sir." Then he stood. "I thank you for your time. I'll join my men now. You'll be needing all the hands you can get today."

"Aye." The other man rose as well. "I'd best get back to it as well."

And the pair went back out into the broken port.

A grim and taciturn Rafe wandered down to the Breakwater Dock to lend his help and his presence to the port's needs, but the conversation with the Lord Mayor rattled him. Something changed under his watch and slipped past his guard. The impossible had happened, and in all likelihood could continue to happen. The captain glanced out to the sea, his home, his comfort.

He shivered.

Chapter Seven
Goodbyes

The *Celestial Jewel* stood anchor outside Llansfoot harbour, overlooking the beach. Rafe leaned against the rail, watching the townsfolk gather driftwood for a bonfire. Watching with him on opposite sides, were Blackthorne and One-Eyed Anders.

"The fire. 'Tis for the memorial?"

"Aye, it is, Anders. Once the sun goes down, they'll light the wood and let the smoke rise to the stars and sea with the departing spirits of their loved ones. There's usually song and prayer as well. It's generally a lovely service."

"But not this time, sir?" Blackthorne's voice added itself to the conversation.

Rafe shook his head. "Too many dead for it to be anything but tainted. Too many dead, and for wrong and unsettling reasons."

Blackthorne ignored the implications of the captain's

remark. "Will you be attending, sir?"

"Aye. I can't in good conscience do otherwise."

"If I'm not needed aboard ship, I'd also like to attend."

"I would too. With your permission, Captain." Anders threw his request into the mix.

"You can both go, and any of the other crew that care to. Ghosts or live souls will be welcome here."

"I'll inform the crew." Blackthorne walked away followed by Anders, leaving Rafe alone with his thoughts, none of which remained happy, most riddled with guilt.

My sister did this. For no better reason than she could, than she wanted to hurt me. Her madness is getting worse. She wants a reckoning.

Rafe gripped the rail, his knuckles turning white. He watched the survivors of Llansfoot collect the driftwood, picking up fuel like the pieces of their broken lives.

The consequences left by gods.

Consequences his sister would see repeated until he stopped her. He sighed.

There's no avoiding a confrontation this time.

Rafe continued to stare at the beach, the sea wind ruffling his hair.

The observance began after dusk as the now waning moon rose and the stars stretched out into infinity. Standing on shore, toe scuffing the sand, Rafe glared at the moon as if it had no right to be overhead. A bit petulant, but the moon was hers. To him, on this night, its light was tainted.

The gathered crowd numbered large with all who lost someone assembled and many more besides. People lined the whole stretch of the beach, well up into the scrub and underbrush and along the path. Rafe scanned the faces. Most of his crew were here, ghosts and the living alike. Including, he noticed, Hugh Corwin who stood with Mouse and half a dozen other ghostly sailors at the edge of the sea. They kept away from the main crowds but seemed respectful of it all.

"The dead will be well honoured." Blackthorne's voice haunted Rafe from the darkness.

"Yes, they will. I suppose there's some comfort in that. And I'm glad the crew's honouring the fallen." Then he nodded towards Hugh. "He's making friends, I hope."

"Aye, in a fashion. He's taken to Mouse. So, that group of quiet misfits who Mouse consorts with have included him. Good lads, so I let it be. Keeps the new one out of trouble at least."

"Some good news, then, and one less worry."

Movement caught his attention, and the captain turned to see the throng part to let the Lord Mayor, the harbourmaster, an aged cleric, and the town elders pass. Each man carried a ship's lantern to light his way and a small scroll. Rafe knew each scroll had the names of the dead written on the parchment. One by one, the procession of men walked to the unlit bonfire and tucked their scrolls in amongst the wood.

Rafe hung back, letting the town elders officiate the ceremony. Some of his crew mingled with the crowd: a bonded blend of the dead and living. Rafe looked upward. The night sky draped wide above him, the half-moon and stars now streaked with clouds. A thousand eyes gazing down to mourn the dead of Llansfoot.

His gaze turned back as the seaport cleric walked to the unlit bonfire holding a burning torch and leaning on a gnarled cane.

"We light this fire for remembrance. We light this fire to speed the journey. We light this fire to show the way home." The man tossed the flaming brand, and it landed perfectly among the piled driftwood. Moments later, the alcohol-soaked wood blazed into fiery life.

Sparks danced like earthbound stars, and the smoke wafted towards the drifting clouds. The pungent scent of the smoke tickled Rafe's nose, and he inhaled deeply. He loved the smell, even on such occasions as this. He raised his head again, staring into the firmament of starlight shining against the black and watched the haze and ash ascend on the night's wind.

From somewhere within the gathered came the strumming of a stringed instrument, and the soft rhythmic thump of a skin drum. Soon the trill of pipes joined in, and the accompaniment of humming voices. In moments, a feminine voice began to sing, with others coming in including, Rafe recognized, Short Davy. Soon, the words of the song filled the space of the beach and reached sweet tendrils out to sea.

My heart, it sings the sea's enthrall.
A sail unfurled, with wind and wave.
Fair sailor's life, those daring brave.
My heart, it sings the sea's enthrall.

A sail unfurled, with wind and wave.
Stars and storms, to death I dance.
Adventure grand, a breath of chance.
A sail unfurled, with wind and wave.

Stars and storms, to death I dance,
and salted tears fill the ocean deep.
That broken rain, that widow's weep.
Stars and storms, to death I dance.

And salted tears fill the ocean deep.
My heart, it sings the sea's enthrall.
Come shine or calm, the rain or squall,
and salted tears fill the ocean deep.

My heart, it sings the sea's enthrall.

A sail unfurled, with wind and wave.
Fair sailor's life, those daring brave.
My heart, it sings the sea's enthrall.

The song engulfed the beach, a chorus of voices linked across the sand raising their goodbyes to the stars, the gods, and the souls of loved ones beyond the mortal world. Harmony swelled building a tidal wave of poignancy until the last note broke and faded into the gentle wind.

Silence settled as all eyes watched the flames crackle and the smoke curl into the darkness. Then the temple's Grand Master stepped forward. Rafe inhaled a sharp breath. He hadn't heard Kyyn would attend.

The Grand Master bent down and grasped a handful of sand, turning to face the crowd. He let the grains slowly trickle from his fingers as the fire illumined his form in an orange glow.

"Such is existence like sand through your fingers flowing fleeting. We cannot stop it. We cannot slow down the end. We only endure." He turned and gestured to the ocean. "From the sea comes life. From the sea comes death. Everything is united in one circle." Then Kyyn clasped his palms together. "When troubles come, we pray. We pray for the peace of our departed brothers and send our hearts with them to the After World. Those beloved are not lost forever, but wait for us to join them." Hesitation cracked through his voice on those words so close to a lie. "May the dead go with solace. May the dead journey without care. We give them back to the sea and the stars. We give them back to the gods."

Behind the crowd, all his gathered priests bowed their heads and chanted:

"We give them back to the sea and the stars. We give them back to the gods."

And then the crowd joined in. "We give them back to the sea and the stars. We give them back to the gods."

Rafe bowed his head but said no words of prayer. He knew the Grand Master's words were well meant but hollow. There would be few souls from this attack waiting in the After World. They were lost. Gone. Devoured by the children of those gods mentioned in empty entreaties and words while the sea and stars watched with indifference.

The gods, *his family*, let this horror happen. He was the only god that cared for the dead.

And he failed to protect them.

Chapter Eight
Incoming Storms

As the night lengthened, the crowds dispersed, the beach settled into quiet, and the bonfire died to glowing embers. A sombre crew drifted back to the ship, lingering on deck, taking solace in each other. Shadows and unspoken words hung against the light from one lantern, the remains of the fire, and the ever-present stars and moon. A hush of uncertainty shrouded the men and the night.

The captain leaned against the rail, a tankard of grog in his hand, and watched Blackthorne hand out more of the liquor to the crew. Silence clung like thick morning fog as men took their portions. None of the usual banter or jokes passed between them. The funereal pall of misery from Llansfoot still chased them.

Captain Morrow raised his drink. "To those lost. And to those they left behind."

A weak chorus of, "Aye. To those lost." rang up from the

crew, but few took a drink. Most only stared into their flagons. A strange unease settled on the ship and didn't look to lifting.

Rafe glanced at the shore and the glowing, charred remnants of the bonfire.

"It doesn't seem natural, does it, boys? Something seems not right, out of order."

A murmur of assent rippled across his men.

"That's because there is something amiss. Trouble's a-brewing. You all can feel it and I know it in my bones. The Moon Goddess has seen fit to fire a shot across our bow, gents. And a terrible, impossible one that hit hard. Now we have to decide what we're going to do about it."

Rafe smiled, soft and cheerless, and casually took a sip of his drink. Then he boomed, "Are we going to cower like fearful children and run from the trouble, or are we going to mourn like men and then take the fight to her? What's it going to be fellows? Are we going to run or fight?"

Rafe gave the assembled a hard glare. He could feel their backs go up at his insinuation of cowardice. For a moment, the deck held calm like a sea with no wind, before One-Eyed Anders stepped forward.

"I can't speak for these lily-livered rascals, but I say fight!" He raised his drink and then downed half of it in one gulp. Behind him more shouts echoed of 'Fight!' and soon the whole crew was drinking and shouting.

The battle cry echoed off the waves, and, for a moment, Rafe fancied the reflecting moonlight shivered.

It gave him hope.

Be afraid, little sister. I'm coming.

The wind rattled the sails in answer.

"Nicely done, Captain." Blackthorn sidled out from the darkness. "How bad is it, truly? Are we in deep?"

"Aye. It's as bad as it gets."

"It's a different game, isn't it? Do we know the rules yet? Or the how?"

"Not yet. But we'll get our answers, Blackthorne. We must."

"Then what, sir?"

Unwilling to answer, Rafe hesitated. Then, spotting Hugh Corwin chatting with Mouse, he quickly changed the subject. "How's our new recruit taking all this mess? You said earlier he was fitting in?"

Blackthorne sighed at the captain's evasion but did not press his question. Instead, he replied dutifully, "Aye. He had some anxious moments, but he did well helping out. Took the killing better than some of the old-timers. Steady as the tide, considering the raw memories he must have of her creatures. Surprised me a bit, he did, after his initial adjustment. But then, he's new enough not to have the sense to worry about what's coming."

"Or still too preoccupied with his own fate." Rafe sighed quietly, not more than a breath of sound. "Do you remember when we were that young and foolish? No cares? No responsibilities?"

"Sir, I'm not certain I ever felt like that."

Rafe stared for a moment and then chuckled. "Come to think on it, I'm not sure I did, either. Aren't we a pair?"

"Indeed, sir. It's probably why we work so well together."

"And someone needs to keep the world running, isn't that right Blackthorne?"

"Aye, Captain. Someone does." Blackthorne gave a nod and a touch of his hat, and slipped back among the crew, leaving Rafe amused.

The efficiency of the man scares me on occasion. He always knows what to say to me. It was a damn lucky day for this ship when he came aboard.

The sound of oars slapping against the water interrupted the night. Rafe turned, and in the lantern's light he caught the silhouette of a boat rowing towards the ship, two shapes huddled in its confines.

He leaned slightly over the rail, and shouted down, "Ahoy the boat! State your business!"

A figure raised an answering hail, "We have urgent news for Captain Morrow and the crew of the *Celestial Jewel*. Permission to come aboard."

His gut knotting in nerves and dread, Rafe barked, "Permission granted!"

He then looked back to the crew, scanning for Blackthorne. The man strode forward without being summoned.

"Get them aboard and send them to my cabin. I'll be waiting." Then he marched past his crew and hurried below deck.

The two messengers arrived minutes later to find Rafe behind his desk with a bottle of rum and three full glasses waiting.

"Sit you two and have a drink to warm your bones."

The two, a sour looking gentleman and a tall, thin woman, settled into chairs and happily downed their rum. They stared into empty glasses. Neither seemed anxious to relay their news.

Rafe took pity on them. "What's happened?"

The woman spit it out, her voice full of anger, fear, and bewilderment. "There've been more attacks! We've gotten word that Pentown and Echo Bay been ravaged. They even tried at Black Shoals, but the cannon there drove 'em off."

Rafe closed his eyes for a heartbeat against reality.
Damn.
"When?"

"Just before sundown." The woman's voice raked anger across the cabin. "The beasts were killing more souls as we were preparing to say goodbye to our dead! I want to gut them all and serve them on a platter!"

"It's an all-out war, then." Rafe chased his whisper with rum and poured himself another glass. "Have the other seaports and islands been warned?"

"Aye, sir." A deeper, masculine croak of a voice replied. "Every spellcaster is up and spreading the word. Telling folks to shore up defences and evacuate inland as much as possible."

"Good. How bad were the casualties?"

"Not as bad as they could have been, but lives were lost." The woman snarled her lips, her voice dripping with venom. "Reports said Pentown's storm wall took the brunt of the destruction but protected the town proper. Same can't be said for two incoming ships. They went down with all hands. Echo Bay's people got word in time and evacuated most beforehand, but the harbour's smashed to ruin. By all accounts, it was the same as here. The creatures moved in, raised havoc, and left."

"Did the towns defend themselves at all? Did the Black Shoals' cannon injure or kill any of the creatures?"

"Aye. They got shots off all right. And the Black Shoals guns killed several by the reports."

"If those reports ain't exaggerated." The man chimed in again. "You know how those Black Shoals people be."

"True, but I'm thinking they were honest enough with this."

Rafe repressed a smile, despite the gravity of the situation. Seaport rivalry never stopped. "Was there anything else?"

"No, sir." The man hesitated, and the woman finished the sentence.

"The Lord Mayor wants to know what you'll be doing about this. Whether you can put a stop to it. So does Abersythe, and the rest."

"Direct. I like that in a woman." This time he did smile, and she blushed. "Tell the ports we set sail with the morning tide, and this matter will be the only thing on our minds. I'll get to the bottom of what's happening, and yes, put a stop to it. If I can."

Mollified, the pair rose, returned their glasses to his desk, and shook Rafe's hand with a, "Thank you, sir." Then they took their leave.

A few minutes later, a knock came at the door.

"Come in, Blackthorne."

The first mate entered with a chuckle. "Am I that predictable?"

"Just that competent."

"The messengers are off the ship and headed back to port. What news did they leave?"

"Nothing good. There have been more attacks at three other ports." Rafe heard a hissing intake of breath, but no other outward sign of shock from his first mate.

He continued. "The beasts apparently took casualties at Black Shoals though, so that may deter my sister for a while. She might lick her wounds for a bit before trying again. We'll sail out tomorrow, survey the damage, collect information, and make a plan of action. We need to start hunting these things down, Blackthorne. And figure out how this is possible."

"It's truly come to that, has it?"

"Yes, old friend, it has. It's worse than I feared. This wasn't an aberration."

"So the spell holding the beasts in check *has* been

broken?" Rafe nodded, and Blackthorne sighed. "Is there no way to fix it? Put them back under restraint?"

"You know as well as I, once a spell's been fractured you can't repair it. And the conditions that led to the original binding were unique. It's unlikely I can recreate them or the spell. The monsters are off their tether, Blackthorne. For good. They're free."

Far away, a mourning dirge crooned on the silver filaments of moonlight and wind. A wild-eyed Goddess of the Moon gyrated on the sand pouring her heartbreak into the night. From the dark sea came answering wails as her children lamented for their lost siblings, and she dropped to her knees, hair the colour of hoar frost brushing against the sand.

She balled her hands into fists and screamed, "You said they'd be free! Not dead! You promised me the chance to end him! To end this pain! Liar!"

Around her, the shadows outside her moonlight quivered, and the air above her turned to mist. The haze coiled and writhed, forming the shape of a huge crow. The bird sailed the air currents, circling ever lower, until it settled on wet sand, the tide touching its feet.

From its coal-black beak, a hoarse voice uttered, "I gave you the spell. You set them free. Your brother holds them in check no longer. I did not lie."

"They were defeated! They were killed! My brother still roams the seas! He will find a way to stop them. To stop me!"

The bird cackled and flapped its wings. "A sorrow, yes, but not a setback. You did what was needed. You did what you do best. Strike out, lash out, hurt, hurt, hurt. Calamity and upheaval. Just enough to sow fear and turmoil to bring another player into the game. She is ready to do her part, lead your brother along the path to where he needs to go."

The Moon Goddess frowned. "Path, what path?"

"To the place for the killing stroke." A cackle and a flap of wing punctuated the words. "Where does your brother hold his power? Where would he be vulnerable?"

The Goddess of the Moon then smiled. "I know, I know. His place. His place of power." She traced a circle in the sand with her finger. "Out in sea, the faraway sea. Where they cross on waves that toss." She laughed, her voice echoing into the night.

The crow hopped about and shook its wings in response. "Yes. That's where you must strike. I tell you true, he will travel there soon and open his doom. You must send your children through."

"Through?" She tossed her arms upward and let out a screeching whoop. "Off on an adventure, yes? To destroy it all!" Her laughter rained down over the beach. "I can take it all away. No more souls, no more worlds, no more brother!" She scooped a handful of sand and tossed it in the air, staring at the crow. "I will send my eldest. He will tear down it all down."

The crow screeched, "No! Send them all through! Attack in force when it's time! Send them all!"

The Goddess scowled and screamed back, "Don't tell me what to do! I'll send who I wish! Do as I wish!"

"Then you will lose! As you always have! Listen to me!" With a strident caw, the crow leapt, his wings catching the air currents. "Send them all! I command you!" The bird soared above the ocean, tossing final words to the glowering figure on the sand. "Oh yes, my Goddess of the Moon, send them all through when I tell you! Rain annihilation on both worlds! Destroy everything! Turn it all to ash!"

Chapter Nine
The Oracle

The ship left the town of Llansfoot the next day with the rising sun. They left behind broken lives and a town in need of rebuilding. Their horizon promised more of the same misfortune as their first task unfurled to investigate the other attacks starting at Black Shoals. As they put to sea, Blackthorne and the captain stood on deck while the sunrise broke in a display of cerise and deep orange.

In contrast to the night before, the first mate seemed agitated, peppering the air, and Rafe, with questions.

"I can't fathom this. If her sea creatures are truly free of your restraints, does that mean they have gone mad, unpredictable in their patterns? Why should the Moon Goddess attack the towns of Pentown, Echo Bay? If her goal is to strike at you, it makes little sense. Neither of them has a temple. And if she's set her sights on the island of Black Shoals we may have other problems. The Royal Navy has a strong presence there and may not overlook this as is their usual habit."

Rafe took a breath. "Excellent points, Blackthorne, but I have little answer to this situation. Before I saw the devastation we left behind, I would have said what happened impossible. Now... I believe unpredictable an apt word, my friend. The very fact she's broken the binding spell somehow is unthinkable." He shook his head. "But as to your opinions on the Royal Navy..." Rafe snorted. "I wouldn't fret over them. They're content to patrol the Seven Kingdoms and let the Outer Islands take care of themselves. If the outgoing cargo ships get attacked, then we might see more of their presence, but they care little for the island settlements. Even the bunch at Black Shoals." He cast a quizzical glance at Blackthorne. "You know that better than anyone."

"Aye, I do. I also know they don't like trouble. Even out here. And trouble's coming. A sticky mess we'll be in the thick of now, won't we?"

"Aye. That goes without saying. We're always in the thick of trouble." Rafe shot Blackthorne a half grin. "But probably not today. So let's put an end to worry, for now, and enjoy the sunrise while we can. It looks to be breaking onto a beautiful day."

The captain's prediction proved correct. The day morphed into a picturesque delight, a luminous illusion pasted over pending calamity. The sea swirled a teal and turquoise, gently undulating as the *Celestial Jewel* bobbed through its glassy surface waves. The wind puffed the sails into full white billows, pushing the ship speedily along its course. Above them, the sun glittered in the azure sky, dancing off the milk pearl, downy clouds.

Rafe walked the deck, breathing in the balmy air with its salted fish crusted tinge and gazing at the ever-stretching horizon.

Even with the world gone mad, there can be days like this. In this, there is hope.

The thought warmed his cockles, and he smiled. A grin to nearly split his face in twain, and a little snatch of a tune formed in his throat, humming its way to his lips. For just a moment he let slip all the threats, all the cares.

What a splendid day to be at sea, and feel the rock of a ship beneath your feet.

But before the thought even cast itself into the wind, the clouds darkened near instantaneously, and a fork of lightning cracked the once blue sky. Rafe froze in his movement, sucking in his breath. The sea to the starboard side boiled and foamed, rising in a great spiralling eruption, shaping into a gigantic waterspout.

"Hard to port! Hard to port!" The shout of Blackthorne echoed off the rigging and Rafe felt the ship shudder. He sighed, and yelled, "Avast! Heave to, lads! We have a visitor and it ain't no use in running!"

As crew jumped to his orders and adjusted the sail to slow down the ship, Rafe watched the waterspout. It hung between water and air, shifting to match the course and sway of the ship. He felt the *Jewel* quiver as the ship tacked, while the crew sheeted the sails and backed the jibs. He waited until the ship's forward momentum slowed, and she eased against the wind.

"Show yourself!" His voice rose among the passing seabirds. "I'm willing to listen, but make it quick! I've things to do and places to be!"

A soft chuckle reverberated out of the churning water. The liquid curved and bent, arcing in close proximity to the sails, always keeping pace with Rafe's ship. Slowly a face appeared within the depth of the moving spout and with a splash, a lithe and beautiful woman landed gracefully on deck. She rose from her crouched position with a smile, covered in naught but a few scant pieces of seaweed.

"Lynna." Rafe grinned, despite everything, seeing the gaping mouths and shocked expressions of his crew. Poor Blackthorne was as red as the setting sun and staring at his toes. "You do know how to make an entrance. But perhaps you might cover yourself while on deck." He shucked out of his coat and handed it to her.

She glared at the garment like it was a three-day-old

fish. "Human conventions are a nuisance, but it is your ship." She took his coat and slipped it over her body. Behind her, some of the crew sighed.

"So what brings the great Goddess of the Sea to my small abode? Something other than sisterly love, I suspect?"

"Of course. No offence brother, but I prefer the briny deeps to the surface. Too much noise up here, I prefer my peace and quiet, and the care of my creatures." She suddenly sighed and scrunched her face in distaste. "Which leads me to why I'm here. Those abominations of the Moon Goddess, our dear sister. They're not in hibernation, they're still active past the full moon! What happened to your binding spell? Something's awry!"

"Why, Lynna, have you come with a friendly warning, then?" Rafe quirked an eyebrow, avoiding the awkward question about his spell. "Not at all like you."

Lynna scowled. "You need to do something! They're stirring currents of turmoil, brother dear, making my darlings afraid to swim freely. And it's not random, either, I can feel it. She's got her hand in this. She's up to something, directing those monsters of hers, planning something terrible. You have to put a stop to it! You have to put aside your hesitation and finally deal with her."

"I already know about her shenanigans, she's attacked one of my temples." Rafe smiled and watched Lynna's placid reaction with a touch of smugness. "But I think you already knew that. What aren't you telling me?"

The sea goddess sighed. "It's not just you. Those beasts of hers rampaged through one of my undersea shrines as well. And..." Lynna stared at Rafe, her voice hesitating. "I don't want this task, but I have a message. Go to the Rock Island Temple. The Oracle wishes to speak with you."

"Does she now?"

"Yes. Your precious acolytes roped me into delivering her request. They didn't care that I don't want to be involved."

"But didn't you say our sister was causing trouble for you? I think perhaps you should take your own advice about hesitation. Stop hiding."

"Don't twist my words!" In a fit of anger, she peeled off Rafe's coat and leapt to the ship's rail. She glared, but added, "I'll try to keep an eye on her beasts, brother, give warning to the humans where I can, but that's the best I can do." With a wave, she dove back into the sea.

Rafe stared past his ship, his gaze lingering on the water, still rippling from her dive. Then he shouted, "You heard her men! Raise the sail and change course for Rock Island Temple!"

The alabaster spires and craggy cliffs of Rock Island silhouetted the horizon from a mile out, and the *Celestial Jewel* glided effortlessly into the harbour the following midday. With a flawless mooring, they dropped anchor at the pristine dock in the quiet port of Blue Bay, the town that lived in the shadow of the great temple.

Standing on deck, the bustle of the crew around him as they docked, Rafe gazed upward at his most grand and famous temple. It dominated the centre of the island, built on a stone rise and ascending to the sky.

The twin pinnacles loomed over the landscape and the commanded the structure: matched, corkscrew domed towers of white rock and brick. Between them stretched an arched, white stone wall and silvery gate, leading—Rafe knew—to a lush garden courtyard. Surrounding this atrium, spread rectangular rows of ornate halls and buildings of a blue and ivory hue. The temple personified peace and sanctuary, constructed to mirror the sea and sky.

And it was home to the Oracle of the Soul.

The woman he was here to see.

Rafe straightened his shoulders and turned to address his crew. "You all have liberty in the port, while I conduct my business at the temple. Try not to tear the place down." He flashed a forced grin, to belay his worry.

Blackthorne cleared his throat to catch Rafe's attention. "Do you want me to accompany you, sir, to the temple?"

Rafe smiled again, this time a genuine one. "A kind offer, but no. It's best I go alone this time."

As soon as the ship was moored and cleared with the

harbourmaster, the captain disembarked. He threaded his way through the dockside market, busy with early afternoon custom. The culture of the islands enveloped him as a dozen dialects chattered around him, mixing with fragrant spices, the pungent fruit of the northern regions, and the tang of fish and sweat. Laughter and hawking patter filled the air, and the lively conversation of neighbours melded with the splash of bright patterned fabrics and shiny trinkets. He slid through the crowds with ease, swift and purposeful, despite the vendors' entreaties to stop and sample their wares.

Once free of the marketplace, he skirted the edge of town, taking the path along the coastal shore, and then uphill to the temple. He could hear the music well before the gates came into his sight, and the scent of the garden's flowers wafted down along the breeze.

Rafe sighed. Part of him wanted to turn back. Get on his ship and sail away. Keep sailing until he put his duties, his sister, all his family really, and his whole life behind him. But he couldn't. He wouldn't do that to the souls in his care. So he moved forward until he stood before the gates to his Rock Island Temple.

He rang the small bell attached to the gate and shouted. "Captain Rafe Morrow seeks an audience with the Oracle of the Soul!"

Almost instantaneously, a figure scurried to approach the gate, a temple noviciate Rafe surmised from the simple way he dressed. He pulled open the gate and then bowed, his close-shaven head level with his knees.

As he rose from the obeisance, he closed the gate behind Rafe. Then—his head still somewhat lowered and his eyes downcast—he whispered, "An honour, Exalted One. The Oracle, she is expecting you. If you would please follow me." He moved a few shuffling steps and glanced back covertly. Rafe suppressed a smile but fell in behind the monk.

The man led Rafe through the beautiful garden, past the summer coral trees and the arbours of creeping vine blossoms, across the fishpond bridge, and along the winding rock bed terrace. They stopped at the private entrance to the oracle's personal chamber.

"She bids you go in alone from here, Exalted One." And with a nod, the novice monk darted off.

For a moment, Rafe paused, tracing the ornate seashell pattern engraved on the door. One moment more of peace before facing whatever troubled waters lay in his path.

Then he turned the handle and entered.

He walked into the shadowy antechamber, illuminated only by the sun streaming from the roof skylight. The aroma of flowery perfume and musky incense infused the air with every breath, and he heard the soft tinkle of wind chimes from somewhere within its depths. He strolled to the next room where the oracle awaited him.

She sat in the middle of a sunlit room, perched in a high-backed velvet chair, rows of windows casting dappled radiance to every corner. The fabric of her throne matched the sea blue shade of her sparkling eyes, and its grand opulence a match with her demeanour. She wore a sleeveless, flowing gown of diaphanous turquoise, belted at the waist, and her dark black hair drifted free across her shoulders.

"Hello, Captain Rafe Morrow." She smiled, her lips more bright and joyful than the daylight. "Or do you prefer Exalted One?"

Rafe snorted. "Most amusing. You know I hate being called that." Then he returned her grin. "It is nice to see you again, Amaratha. I wish it were under better circumstances."

"As do I. But life never allows us to choose. It always surprises."

"More like a gut punch, I'd say."

She chuckled. "Perhaps. Perhaps not. I think the outcome of this depends on much, God of Souls, and not just on your actions."

"So you have had a vision. Was it of her, the Moon Goddess? Do you know what she's planning? How she's done the impossible?"

A sorrow crossed her face, shading the sunshine. "I have seen glimpses, yes, of how and why, and of shadows on wings. I've seen terrible death images where the sea is as red as the blood. Your sister's madness consumes her as always, but something else goads her, aids her in these new attacks. That I know."

Rafe frowned, impatience simmering past his outer facade. "Do you know how to stop her? That's all I care about."

"Is it now?" Her tone tossed back a rebuke. "Then you are short-sighted, oh great Exalted One. The path to resolution is not solitary. Stopping her will come only if you remember who she truly is, Captain." the Oracle leaned forward. "I have seen one path to her redemption, her peace. You will have a choice at the end of your long battle. Make the right one. Don't let pride and anger stand in the way of her salvation. That choice may have lasting consequences."

Bewilderment filled Rafe. "Why would I want to stand in the way of my sister's peace? The end to her storm born chaos is what I want."

"Emotions are a strange thing, Captain. Capricious. And as I said, she is not alone in this. One decision may topple worlds."

A chill ran through his bones, like a winter wind across his bow. "How very ominous."

"More than you realize." She smiled again. "Come sit, we will have tea, and I will tell you everything I saw." She waved her delicate fingers at a nearby chair and rang a small silver bell for her attendant. A girl materialized from an adjacent room. "Bring us some tea. A blend from the Wakeford Islands, I think."

With a nod and a bow, the girl hurried off, and Rafe pulled up a chair and sat down.

"Lynna visited me. She said you sent her."

Amaratha laughed. "I did. She didn't like it either. But I feel Lynna's... involvement may be necessary later."

"You planning on telling me why?" Rafe leaned back in his chair. "Sometime today would be nice."

"I will. But these things are best discussed over tea." She folded her hands demurely and refused to say another word until her servant brought in a tray weighted with two cups, milk, and a steaming pot of tea. The girl poured the hot liquid for her mistress and guest, her hand and body shaking, and then quickly fled.

Amaratha seemed amused by the girl's behaviour. "I do believe you make my attendant nervous, Captain Morrow."

He shrugged. "I seem to have that effect on most temple neophytes, even some aged priests. I've gotten used to it."

"I suppose you have. Does it get any easier, living as you do after this many years?"

Rafe picked up his cup, inhaling the scent of tea, and then answered. "No."

"A shame. For my tidings will not lessen your burdens." Amaratha joined Rafe, scooping her cup into her hands.

"I didn't expect they would. Whatever game the Goddess of the Moon is playing, it is not for the good of this world."

"No, it is not." She took a sip of tea. "She plays the game of death that one, and annihilation. Though I am not sure she understands the whole. Or is simply past caring. The visions her actions have engendered..." Amaratha shuddered.

"Tell me."

She hesitated, staring into her cup. Then her sweet voice lilted soft words. "I saw two worlds, this one and the one beyond. Bleak, cold, full of grey and dust. Husks and empty shells, no light, no life. Only broken gods and empty seas remained. The skies rained ash, and the ground spread cracked and black."

She raised her head, a wild, haunted look burning in her eyes. "I saw the worlds consumed, Rafe, the whole structure of existence gone. She lashes out in her anger, but on the behest of... another. The magic she now wields, the consequences of using it will leave nothing."

So, it has come to this, my sister. A chill quaked under his skin. "How will this happen? What events will put this ending into motion?"

Amaratha sighed. "I don't know. That I didn't see. Just glimpses." She suddenly leaned across and grabbed his hand. "But I know something's crept out of the darkness, Captain, something ancient, older even than your kind. A creature of shadows and sea, of black wind and death. Its mark is on the magic that set her children free of your restraints." She released his hand and leaned back in her chair. "All I saw was a vision of the portal in the sea. You, your ship, and... Your answers may be there, I think." She sighed, a sound delicate like rustling lace. "And, Rafe, warn the temples. They must guard the souls and the portals. And let any souls who wish to leave this world go. They will be safer in the After World. For now."

"She means to confront me then, at last?"

"I fear so, yes. Aided by this other... thing."

Rafe put down his cup, his tea untouched. "I can't worry about whoever's pulling her strings. Not now. She's still controlling her beasts and they're the biggest threat at the moment. Do you know what her next move will be? Where she will strike next?"

"Go to the portal before the next full moon. That's all I was given." Her face cast a grim expression. "I fear, if you do not go, the worlds will turn to obsolete dust, Captain Morrow, and there will be no souls left to call you god."

Rafe sighed. "Very well. I'll play my part. The game will start and end as the fates wish." He rose and gave Amaratha a nod farewell. "May I come again, Oracle, under better circumstances."

He turned on his heel and made his slow path back to his ship.

High in a tree, overlooking a moonlit beach, the

Nightmare Crow cawed. It leapt into the air and soared downward on the air currents to land on the warm sand at the feet of a goddess.

"He's coming. He will be where we wish very soon. A matter of days."

The Moon Goddess looked at the bird, a scowl on her face. "How do you know?"

"A sad little Oracle told me. Or rather I told her. A vision here, a vision there, and who's to know where it came from? Not her. Not her."

She smiled. "He comes because you called, little bird?"

"Yes. Because I called. We called. He will come to watch the destruction. He comes to die. Are you ready?"

"Yes. I have been ready for years. My brother will finally pay for what he did to me."

Chapter Ten
The Portal

Three days hard sailing saw the *Celestial Jewel* hard-pressed with a weary crew. She navigated into the port of every primary Soul Temple in the Outer Islands to spread the Oracle's message of vigilance, and relay the communication by spellcaster to the smaller sanctuaries on the peripheral islands in the western seas. Rafe's presence softened the apprehension as the priests were asked all to facilitate the passage of souls to the After World, but disquiet still sliced across his visit. As more temples and towns became aware, dark clouds of misgiving shadowed the God of Souls and goodwill trickled away like spring rain into summer.

Rafe heard grumblings in the crew about it, but Blackthorne voiced the opinion out loud. "Ungrateful wretches. What do they expect? It's not as if you're responsible for the attacks. Damnation, you're trying to unravel the whole mess."

"They're frightened. And a god they can see is easier to blame than one who's no closer than moonlight. And her sea creatures are still attacking ships. Though no more settlements thankfully."

"Fear is no excuse to turn on the person willing to protect them."

"Perhaps not, but I understand it."

Yet, despite his words, Rafe took to brooding, standing at the prow as the ship sliced through the waves. Only after the last temple visit, did he give the final order.

"We sail to the Sea Portal, boys. An unknown rendezvous awaits us."

Neither cheer, nor smiles met his order as the crew's mood lingered sombre, but the course was laid and the ship cruised from port toward deeper seas. Rafe's gaze left the crew and circled out to stare at the horizon.

"Sir." A soft voice echoed behind him. Rafe turned around to see Hugh Corwin standing there.

"Yes, sailor. What is it?"

"Trouble's coming, isn't it? For left behind souls like me? That's why we're visiting temples along the coast? And you're ordering the souls to pass over, what will go."

"I'm not exactly ordering, but, yes. Trouble's brewing and it will be safer for such as you to be in the After World." Rafe cocked his head. "Why do you ask?" Although he felt he knew Hugh's answer.

"I've been thinking, maybe I should've gone. That I

shouldn't have stayed at all. That my being here was a big mistake." Hugh hung his head, staring at the deck, scuffing wood with his toe. "It didn't seem real. None of this. Not until... recent events. Now I'm scared. I think I'm somewhere I don't belong." He looked up at Rafe, a yawning unhappiness swirling in his eyes. "The crew scuttlebutt is I can use this Sea Portal? Can you put me where I do belong, sir?"

Rafe smiled. "Yes, sailor, I can. Where we're headed, that will put things right for you. You can most definitely pass through the Sea Portal into the After World."

An expression of relief, gratitude, and peace settled in Hugh's face. "Thank you, sir." He looked up at the floating white clouds. "Pretty things those clouds, all fluffy, in the shapes of the animals I remember from my childhood."

"Yes, they do look a bit like animals. Very lovely. In fact, this whole day is lovely." Rafe suddenly smiled and gazed at the horizon. The sun beat down on the sea, casting a silver sheen against the water's surface. The cresting waves sparkled as day stars, shining back up to the sky. A small light of hope re-ignited in his soul.

Hugh matched the Captain's good spirits. "Yes, sir. Such a beautiful day, even a dead man can appreciate it." He grinned at Rafe, who chuckled.

"Cheeky lad. But you're right. The sea's at her best on days like this. Calm, sunny, a lovely sky. With the horizon stretching out to adventure and new destinations.

The best kind of day there is, a day like this."

"Will it be like this after I cross? With a sea, and the salt air?" Hugh sighed. "I'd miss the sea."

"Don't worry. There are seas of all kinds and woodlands, meadows, and mountains. The place shapes itself to your heart, Hugh. If you want a sea, you'll have a sea. In fact, you'll have the perfect sea. With the bluest water and the loveliest of skies. You've nothing to fret about." Rafe tossed him a smile. "You'll see."

"It sounds lovely. And I'll be glad of an end to it, this uncertainty and despair I've been feeling. Aimless I've been feeling, drifting like, as if I have no purpose anymore. I guess it's hard for the dead to have purpose."

"You'd be surprised what can motivate the dead. But I'm glad you've come to acceptance."

"I have. Time to leave my life behind and consent to being dead." Hugh gave a chuckle. "Funny that. Always thought when you died all your choices went away, all the difficult decisions. I guess not."

"Life and death are a mite more complicated I'm afraid."

"Seems so. So how does it work? This passing over?"

"We're headed east, past the islands, out to deeper sea to a place where the configuration of worlds settles just right. I would have taken you there in due course, had you made this decision under normal circumstances. It's where all the souls from this boat pass through." Rafe gave half a smile, half a shrug. "The portal there is under my direct control. I'll open it and create a bridge. You simply have to walk from the ship to the After World like a stroll on a summer's day."

"A simple stroll. A lovely thought." Hugh stared at Rafe for a minute, a strange mix of emotions flitting across his face. Then he turned away and whispered. "Thank you."

Rafe placed a friendly hand on his shoulder. "Everything will be fine."

Come tide and morning light, the ship rolled to their destination a day or so out of Black Shoals. Heading in they heaved to and dropped the sea anchor, letting the *Celestial Jewel* drift on the sea. Rocked by the gentle waves, the crew gazed out at the well familiar position and place.

Then, as routine, Blackthorne shouted a customary refrain. "Dropped anchor at the Sea Portal and awaiting captain's orders!"

Rafe smiled inwardly, though his solemn expression changed not à whit. He took comfort in the words and his crew. "At ease, men, but be vigilant. We are here not only to see off the newest member of this crew," Rafe nodded to Hugh, "but at the behest of the Oracle. She directed us here for answers to our current troubles, and though I see naught but sea at the moment," a few suppressed chuckles sprinkled the air at these words until Rafe gave a glare to the assembled, "I'm certain her insight will reveal itself in due time."

Rafe then beckoned Hugh to his side. "However, we first must bid farewell to our shipmate and comrade. A fine crew member even if he joined us for a short while. To Hugh Corwin! May he find peace in death!" A cheer went up through the rigging and echoed Rafe's words.

"Peace in Death! Peace in Death!"

The sound of their voices lifted above the clouds and spiralled far below the waves. It reverberated off the past and spun out towards the future, carried on souls already crossed and those waiting yet to die.

Rafe paused until the air quieted again, and then stepped away from Hugh towards the rail. The gathered men parted, giving him a clear view of the sea. As Rafe took a breath, a shadow flickered over the deck and the wind hit the sails like the sound of wings. Rafe looked up. A crow circled in the sky far above the ship.

"Something wrong, sir?"

Blackthorne's voice brought Rafe's attention back to earth. "No. Nothing." He shrugged and began the ritual.

"Upon this day we give our brother back to the world beyond. To the arms of those he loved, whose journey ended before his. I call to them to meet his passage, to bring him through to their embrace. What the sea claimed, the sea will now grant peace."

The words fell off his tongue with practised ease, disappearing into the swirling wind. Rafe lifted his right hand, palm side down, splaying his fingers and arching his wrist slightly. A smile lifted the edge of his mouth as he felt the power stir, and slowly a silver-blue glow drifted across his skin, sliding from his fingertips. His thoughts glided with the radiance, wafting, searching past the waves and breeze until the recognizable connection clicked.

Well beyond the ship the waves bounced and twisted, and the sweet scent of spring flowers hit the wind. An answering luminescence glimmered in the air and skimmed the tumultuous water, growing, spreading, until a glistening translucent circle of blue frost formed between the sky and the sea. The gaping hole connecting worlds shifted and shimmered, yawning wide enough to sail the ship through. Another cheer rose among the crew, and the captain heard a gasp from Hugh.

His hand quivered, the energy building, and Rafe twisted his wrist slightly. A flash of light erupted, shooting outward in a starburst, arching over the deck to hover at the rail. Rafe snapped his finger closed, balling his hand into a fist, and a bridge of light snaked across the water from the ship to the portal. It widened, translucent and luminescent, and hovered effortlessly as a connection between the *Jewel* and the After World.

"Anytime you are ready, Hugh. Walk across the

bridge and into the portal. You'll feel some resistance as you cross the threshold, but that's normal."

"Aye, Captain." Hugh saluted Rafe and tossed him a cocky grin even though his voice held tremors. He slowly walked to the rail, ready to climb onto the bridge crossing. Yet, before he could put a foot off the deck, a shout broke through the ceremony.

"What in all the seas!"

A horrendous roar followed the sound of Pinky's voice, and the sea to the far starboard side of the ship erupted in roiling waves and plumes of spray. Then, another shout shocked fear through every man on deck.

"Kraken!"

The cry of terror rose from the ship as surely as the dreadful tentacled, multi-eyed, fang-toothed beast ascended from the depths. The monster uncoiled and swung a colossal appendage, casting a great shadow over the *Jewel*.

"Prepare for incoming!" Rafe shouted a warning and then a command, "Man the sails and hoist the bloody sea anchor!"

But the massive limb did not touch the vulnerable ship. Instead, it smashed it down across the magical bridge. The delicate connection shattered, sending energy and sea slamming against the ship. The vessel lurched, the still set anchor strained, and the crew went tumbling haphazardly head over foot. Rafe felt the surge of backlash blast into his chest, rolling him across the deck to crash into the bulkhead. The wind and magic knocked out of him, he slumped in a heap.

"Captain's down!" Blackthorne's anguished cry chilled the crew even more than the sight of the great beast sloshing through the water, bearing towards the ship.

Chapter Eleven
Kraken

"Man the guns! Man the bloody guns! And hoist that bloody anchor before that bloody beast uses it to drag the ship about!"

Blackthorne's order cut through the panic and crew scrambled to obey. The clattering chain signalled the rise of the anchor while men rushed below decks to prepare the cannon as more leapt to load and aim the deck side harpoons. The first mate clambered to the captain's side with a prayer for both Rafe and what seemed a hopeless situation for the ship. Blackthorne felt a pulse in his commander's wrist and saw the rise and fall of his breath. He sighed with relief and then turned to face his enemy.

But the expected attacked never came.

Instead, the Kraken swam past, bouncing the ship near capsized as Anders wrestled to hold her firm. The monster of the sea barreled straight for—"The Portal! It's attacking the portal!" Outrage sliced the sky as Anders' voice yelled the warning.

"Fire the harpoons! Stop the beast!" The words came quick from Blackthorne's mouth, and swifter still the missiles sped through the air at the creature. They hit true, puncturing the beast's side, tearing scaly flesh in a crimson spurt of fresh blood. It bellowed in pain but charged straight at the open, yawning portal.

Anders wheeled the ship around as the beast hurtled itself through the water, its tentacles flailing at the portal, sparks and radiance flashing against the sea and sky like a violent storm.

Blackthorne's shout of "Fire all weapons" brought another round of harpoons, and this time, cannon fire, which drove the monster off course, but only briefly. With a screech of rage, it advanced on the ship, bent on destruction.

"Ring the damn bell!"

Rafe's voice shouted hoarse, and he grabbed Blackthorne's arm. "Help me stand." The first mate complied, helping Rafe to shaky feet. A scurry of flesh rushed past, and Mouse, with a shaking hand, clanged the ship's bell with all his might.

Sky, breath, wind, and sea all shattered with the echo of the bell, breaking into a thousand bits, and slamming back together. The ship shook as if in the teeth of a storm, and every man aboard screamed from somewhere dark and primal. The clouds blackened and spit rain, while the great Kraken screeched a roar to be heard by the gods themselves.

The beast stopped dead in the water.

The captain fell to his knees and sucked in an agonizing breath, Blackthorne tumbling beside him. His ears filled with noise: the beast's screams, the moans of the crew, and the strange distressed caw of a crow. Rafe cried out against the backlash and mustered all his strength, willing himself to his feet. He stumbled to the rail to see the creature lashing the portal with its tentacles yanking itself towards the opening.

"No!" Rafe summoned all his magic, squeezed every ounce from his being, and formed a seething ball of energy between his hands. He heaved it at the monster, striking it with the force of a hurricane, lifting the creature half out of the water, and thrusting it well beyond the portal.

A sound of shrieking woven with a high whine shattered the area. Such a pitiful, painful sound emanating from the beast. Rafe raced forward, standing boldly at the bow of his ship, anger laced with ferocity on his face and in his blood. The magic sparked off of him, from fingertip to hair follicle.

Rafe shouted defiance from the deck of the ship, hands flung to the skies, voice booming with the shock of thunder. "Away, vile Kraken! This is my domain! Neither you nor my sister have power here!"

The portal light shimmered, cracked, the silver light

shattering into black. In an instant, the gateway between worlds vanished.

"I am God of Souls! You shall not defile this sacred place! Away you vile miscreant spawn!"

The seas around the Kraken boiled, lifting the beast from the ocean in a gargantuan plume of water. Tentacles waved helplessly and it roared its displeasure in a swell that brought the crew to its knees.

Rafe did not flinch. "Tell my sister I am neither weak nor dead! And I will not tolerate this ignominy! There will be a reckoning!"

With a wave of his hand, Rafe hurled the beast through the heavens, cast it against the horizon, and banished it far from the place of the After World portal.

His arms fell to his sides, fists curled. He heard Blackthorne's footsteps behind him.

"How dare she?"

"I don't know, sir. But you took care of the beast. The Sea Portal is safe."

"Is it? Knowing her, she'll try again." Rafe turned his head to stare at the ocean, the spot where a few moments before the door to the After World pulsed. Then he slumped against Blackthorne, all energy spent.

"Help me below deck."

The first mate lent him support, and the pair walked below deck without another word. Dread chased Rafe's footsteps, and a shiver creaked through the bones of the ship.

While far beyond the *Jewel*, and deep below the sea, the Kraken moaned, the anguished cry sliding along the currents to the ears of its mother. Above it all, a crow circled unsteadily in the sky.

Chapter Twelve
Decisions

Blackthorne knocked gently on the door on the captain's quarters. A half hour had passed since Rafe banished the Kraken and left the deck, leaving behind a gaped mouthed and confused crew. More than enough time for recovery and rest.

At the silence, Blackthorne knocked again. As loathe as he was to disturb him, the crew's disquiet could no longer be ignored. They needed their captain. Drifting aimlessly alongside the portal would not do, nor would the crew's unease that rippled throughout the ship. And poor Hugh, pondering his fate, unsure if he would go or stay, did nothing but stare into the water.

Another knock, this time followed by an entreaty. "Captain. Captain Morrow. The crew need orders." Blackthorne kept his voice soft not knowing the man's mood. As fair as he was, the captain's temper could be volatile.

A moment's more silence and then, "Enter."

Blackthorne opened the cabin door with the old familiar creak of its hinges, breaking the silence. Captain Morrow sat behind his desk in his favourite chair staring out the rounded glass of the port window. He didn't bother to glance in Blackthorne's direction as he entered.

"So the crew want orders? They want their stalwart captain to come save the day? Come tell them what to do? Tell them that everything will be all right… Is that it?"

"Yes, sir."

"What if he can't? What if he doesn't know if all will be well?"

"Then he lies, sir. He tells them whatever they need to keep them calm and safe."

"Well, that would truly be a grand lie, I think. I'm not sure there is a safe anymore."

"Sir?"

Slowly, Rafe turned and stared at Blackthorne. The first mate blanched and nearly took a step backward. The expression on his captain's face showed a blistering reflection of pain, rage, and something akin to desolation.

"The Oracle told me something dark was behind all this, Blackthorne. Something ancient and black. I didn't heed, but I think I tasted it out there. Just a touch of something foul. Full of hatred and familiarity. I don't know what it means, but I do know it cannot be allowed into the After World." Rafe reached out and fingered a small box on his desk before opening it. He extracted a smooth black stone. "Do you know what this is, Elliot?"

Blackthorne, more than a bit surprised at being addressed by his first name, could do no more than shake his head.

"It's black amber. A potent thing indeed, this tiny stone. You want me to tell them something comforting. And what if there is no comfort? What if the whole world's gone mad and your captain may have to do something drastic to protect it?"

"Then tell them that. Tell them something. The truth, lies, a blend of both. Whatever comes out of your mouth, just say it. Get up on deck and be our captain." The last words came out of Blackthorne's mouth in a heated rush and made Rafe straighten his spine. In spite of everything, the corner of the captain's mouth quirked.

"Perhaps you should be the one giving the orders, Blackthorne."

"No, sir! Forgive me if I've overstepped, but this isn't the time for wallowing in self-pity or despair. I'm sure there'll be time later, but we're needing action now, sir."

Rafe flinched slightly at the subtle rebuke. "You're correct. And you didn't overstep. Gave me a much needed kick in my backside, more like." Rafe rose to his feet, pocketing the stone. "It's past time I addressed the crew and broke the bad news."

Rafe gave Blackthorne a woeful smile and walked out of his cabin, leaving the first mate to trail after him. Soon after, the pair arrived on deck before a subdued and apprehensive crew.

Blackthorne moved past Rafe to join the assembled. Everyone stared at their captain, expectant and waiting. Rafe felt the weight of his obligations, the horror, and the stark reality shackled him as sure as if he were chained in iron. There could be no escape. Not for the God of Souls, and the captain of the *Celestial Jewel*. Rafe closed his eyes, took a deep inhale, and let out the breath. Then he opened his eyes, turning the full fierce smouldering gaze of a god onto his crew and the world.

"We're at war. This attack by my sister is her declaration. She isn't going to end it here. This loss won't stop her. She'll try again, come back to strike at the portal, attack the temples, perhaps even try and destroy the After World. I know her and her madness. She is single-minded. Her course now set, she will advance on these places repeatedly and with ever greater numbers. She has made her intentions clear. This is what the Oracle foresaw."

He let his words wash over his men, the lies of omission, of what else waited out there scalding at his soul. He let the gasps subside before continuing. "What happens, whatever the outcome from here, I know one thing: I cannot allow her creatures access to the After World. I cannot put every soul there at risk." He paused knowing his next words would shock. "The Sea Portal must be sealed! I will close this gateway After World and all access will be denied! This action will reverberate throughout every portal in the land, and no souls will cross until this fight is finished! The portals remain closed until we are victorious!" A silence, deeper than ever witnessed, fell. Rafe felt the shock and sorrow in his blood. "It must be done. This portal, all portals, must be sealed." He turned to Hugh. "I'm sorry. I can't grant you the peace you seek."

Hugh raised his chin. "After what I've witnessed sir, I understand. I'm with you, no matter what."

Rafe nodded in respect, hiding his surprise.

"You men can stay to watch the spectacle or go below deck. What's about to happen here is heartbreaking, and I'll not think less of you if you'd prefer not to bear witness."

There were murmurs, but not a single man removed himself from deck. The solidarity gave Rafe strength. He walked to the rail, the crew parting to give him a path. He slid a hand into his pocket, closing his finger around the black amber. He extracted the rock, outstretched his hand, and opened his fingers. The stone sat warm and waiting on his palm.

Rafe Morrow closed his eyes. He summoned the magic that flowed inside him, the insubstantial essence that pervaded his flesh and his blood, letting it seep through to his skin. The luminescent magic glowed a pale blue, tinged with ivory and silver, invading the small polished rock in Rafe's hand. Obsidian coils of energy slithered from the dark amber, wrapping themselves around the captain's fingers and arm. Cerulean and midnight aura quivered and melded, and Rafe reached out to connect with the portal.

The customary sensation hit him like a gale wind, like a familiar ache ready to be split open to the world. This time there would be no gateway, no welcome breech to bridge two worlds. With a quick movement of his fingers, he fed the black amber's magic into the hidden portal, slamming the doorway shut and sealed. A scream born of the dark ocean fathoms and the endless sky reverberated across the ship, across the sea. Every man, dead or alive, shivered at the sound.

Rafe let his magic die away and fade back to dormant. The light disappeared, and the black amber sat cold and inert on his palm. He slipped the rock back into his pocket.

"Well, it's done. For good or ill. It's done." A hollow pit squirmed at the bottom of Rafe's gut, threatening to ingest him whole. His bones ached, and he felt exhausted. He needed some quiet. "Set patrols for the next hour to guard against repercussions. Report to me if anything strange occurs or in an hour. Whichever comes first. I'll be in my cabin."

He tried to smile, but only managed a grimace before retreating to the sanctuary of his quarters.

"What have you done?" The Nightmare Crow screeched from its circling flight, with a rage powerful enough to shake the treetops. "You sent one beast! One! I commanded all attack! All!" The bird screamed, chasing the clouds across the moon. "You let him defeat you!"

Below on the sand, the Goddess of the Moon snarled back, "They would not go! They were afraid! Afraid of him and his ship! Only my eldest was brave!"

"You should have made them go! Every one! You failed me!"

"Liar! Liar! You are the one that failed! You were there! My eldest saw you! Told me! Why didn't you fight him! Stop him!" She bared her teeth as if to eat the bird. "But he hurt you! Didn't he? With his bell! I see the signs. Hurt you like you hurt my children! Sent them to do your mischief! Serves you right." She snorted.

"You stupid, foolish creature! Don't you understand? We've lost our chance! He has closed the portals! All of them!"

"What do I care of portals or of you? You are like all the rest! You promised to end my pain! You lied! Go yourself to my brother, you filthy bird, and fight your own battles! Leave me! Leave this place with your lies!"

Another screech and the bird swooped down, skimming past her face before settling to land on a rock near the sea. "I would if I could, *Goddess.*" It spat her title from its beak like a piece of rotten fish. "But I need a surrogate to do my bidding. You were the best I could find. Not good enough, it seems. Not good enough."

The Goddess turned and glared. "Bidding! What a useless thing, that word. I do no one's bidding. I am done with you." She turned her back on the creature and traced patterns in the sand.

"Did I hurt your feelings? Make you angry?" Squawking laughter shrilled over the beach. "It matters not, Goddess, for I am not done with you."

She turned back, still glaring. "Silly thing. Your wishes do not matter to me. You treat me like I was nothing. Come to me with promises and then blame. Like all the rest. No good to me. Be gone." She chuckled. "What can you do to me, little bird? Hurt me? That's been done. Kill me? I welcome it. Any pain you can give me, I already suffer worse. Go away, lying bird. Go away."

The bird ruffled its feathers and pecked at the stone. Silence roosted for long moments, and the crow became as still as death. Then it spoke, its tone less harsh. "Perhaps you are right. Perhaps I have wronged you, spoken out of turn." The crow hopped off the stone and walked closer. "I was angry. I am sorry."

The Goddess of the Moon snorted. "Doubt it. Your kind is never sorry. No more lies."

The bird tilted its head. It laughed, a harsh,

bone-aching sound. "Very well. Truth. I do not care for you, and you do not care for me. But we want the same thing: to end the reign of the God of Souls."

"We tried. We lost. He won." The Goddess scowled. "He always wins."

"No one always wins. Luck turns. And that is what he is, lucky." The creature flapped its wings and walked a circle around the Goddess. "We need to break his luck. A new approach, perhaps. One plan lost, another to rise from its ash." The crow gave a small hop, inching closer to the Moon Goddess. "Now why did we fail? That is the question."

"Easy, silly bird. You lied. You told me you could give me the power to hurt him. You didn't. You are not as strong as he. Not strong at all."

"Not strong... Why you impudent little worm!" The crow's feathers ruffled and it stretched its wings. "I gave you enough power to..." The creature abruptly quieted, the words left unspoken. "Give you power. Perhaps that's it. The missing piece." The crow bobbed its head. "Before, we sent your children. Gave them the task of destroying him. A flawed strategy perchance, doomed to fail."

The Goddess sneered, but the crow ignored her.

"Your beasts are powerful, but simple-minded creatures. Not enough hatred and too much fear to sustain them. You, on the other hand..." A caw and cackle shuddered across the air. "I should have sent you from the start. You, who is potent enough to kill him."

The Goddess smiled. "Now that, little bird, is the first thing you've said that I have found interesting."

"I thought it might be. Not as destructive as my first plan, but it will suffice, nonetheless." The bird stepped even closer. "Hold out your arm." She did as she was asked, and the crow leapt onto the limb. In an instant, it dug its claws into her appendage and slashed her flesh repeatedly with its beak. The Goddess of the Moon screamed and lashed out trying unsuccessfully to dislodge the bird. Moments later, after bloody runes were scored deep into her flesh, the crow flew back to its rock, trailed by her curses.

"What did you do to me, filthy beast!"

"Gave you a gift. Let the cuts heal for a day. Then you can take what you want. Fight him, and with those symbols, you will match his power. Your magic will be as strong as his. You can finally meet him in battle and win."

"How?" She tilted her head, and her anger gave way to a look of curiosity. "No god but my father ever bested him."

"With power older than the gods. The symbols I imparted to you allow you to reach it, use it. It will rise through your own magic for you to control."

A crooked little smile snaked across her face. "My father does such a thing. But not like this. Not runes, and scars and pain. His talisman is a stone with spells and rituals to control what he wills." She stared, her smile turning into a soft giggle. "Who are you, little crow?"

The crow chortled, a hoarse shrill noise, but only answered, "I know all about your father's talisman. The thing he holds over all his children. Who do you think gave it to him so many years ago?"

With another cackling laugh, the crow took flight, leaving the Goddess of the Moon, staring at the bloody lacerations in her arm.

Chapter Thirteen
Soundings

A knock sounded on the door of the captain's quarters. Rafe raised his head from the glass of wine he nursed.

"Come in." As much as he might wish, there was no use hiding from it.

Blackthorne entered. Rafe found his stern countenance a strange comfort.

"I've come with a report, sir. It's been an hour since…" He let the sentence trail off and stared at his boots for a moment.

Rafe nodded, avoiding the sight of his first mate's uneasy countenance. "Anything out of the ordinary? Any more creatures?"

"No, sir. It's been smooth sailing and calm seas. We conducted short patrols of the area, but nothing, sir. Did the crew some good, though. A bit of routine composed their nerves."

"That's something at any rate." Rafe stared out the porthole. "Have the crew set a course back to the nearest port and then come join me for some wine."

Silence hung for a moment in the room. "Very well, sir."

Blackthorne retreated, and, within minutes, Rafe felt the ship lurch and shift course. Rafe pulled an additional glass from his cabinet and set it next to the decanter on his desk. A few moments after that, another knock sounded on the door.

"Enter."

Blackthorne appeared and sat down in a nearby chair. Rafe poured him a glass of wine and handed it to his first mate. Blackthorne took the offering and settled back in his chair with a sigh.

"A right mess, isn't?" Rafe tossed a wry smile. "I keep wondering how it got to this state." He imbibed a large sip of wine. "It doesn't seem..." Rafe submerged his words in more wine, before continuing in a more melancholy tone. "Never envy the gods, my friend. Our lives offer little but endless days and regrets." Rafe gulped the last remains of wine in his glass and poured himself another.

"How much wine have you had, sir?"

"Not enough, Blackthorne. Not enough."

The first mate swirled his own glass of alcohol. "I suppose today, if any, is a good day to drown one's sorrows."

"It is, but I fear there will be others. Worse ones. Ones all the wine in the kingdoms won't drown." Rafe sighed long, weighty, and ugly. "It wouldn't be so painful, so difficult, what's coming, if I didn't remember."

"Remember, sir?"

"The times before, when we weren't so burdened with years and discontent. She used to dance, my sister. Did you know that?"

Blackthorne shook his head.

"She did. Along the cliffs and the beaches, across the seas, under the pale light of her moon. She was beautiful then. Carefree, happy, and kind. I miss her kindness. Sometimes, long ago, she was the only one who was kind to me."

"And now?" Blackthorne's quiet voice sliced the strain of the room as well as any sword.

"And now I'll most likely have to destroy her. Or she and this power that's using her will destroy all of us. I'll have to kill her or break her, Blackthorne. One way or another, I'll have to sever her power as a goddess." Rafe raised his glass in salute. "To the games gods play. Damn them all, and may we win."

Blackthorne raised his glass, and they both drank, the wine consumed in one swallow. For a moment, they stared in silence, each lost in their own thoughts, then Rafe sighed.

"I suppose half drunk or not the crew needs orders." He rose, wobbling a little on his feet. "So, do you think they'll listen to a slightly inebriated captain?"

Blackthorne snorted. "Those lot? They'd ask for a share of the wine."

Rafe laughed softly. "They would at that." The captain moved around the desk. "Come on then. Let's get on deck. We have sailing to do and a goddess to stop."

Blackthorne rose as well, questions tumbling past his lips before his good sense could stop it. "Sir, what will be the repercussions of this? What are we facing besides the coming battle with your sister?"

Rafe looked pained. "I don't know, Elliot. I truly don't. What I did will reverberate through every portal. They are all closed now. How the priests, the people will react to that, well, I suspect it will not pass with good grace."

"What will it mean? For the dead?"

"Death will continue. People will still die, and most will pass on as customary. The rest, they'll linger or be eaten by my sister's children until the portals reopen. The world has changed, Blackthorne. I think we will be facing fear, my friend."

Blackthorne nodded, a saddened expression on his face. They both stared for a moment lost in their thoughts, and then returned topside.

The day still spread beautiful across the horizon as they emerged from below deck, the brilliant sunshine beckoning to possibilities. Despite what occurred, the blue sky had not torn asunder, the sea did not rage, and the call of the seabirds echoed in the distance. The world still lived, and work still lay ahead.

"The day's not done, boys." Rafe's voice boomed,

words cutting across the warm sunshine and air like the prow of his ship through water. "There's sailing yet to be had today, and more hard days to come. We have been called to war whether we want it or not. Set course, Mr. Anders, back to the nearest island temple. We'll be checking in there as the first port of call."

"Aye, sir. That'd be Black Shoals Temple. Laying in course, sir."

He adjusted the helm and the ship's bones creaked as it turned towards the islands. In its wake, it left churning seas and finality. On its horizon, an uncertain future.

⚓

The return trip from the outlying ocean began in dismal temper, but a few hours into sailing with salt air and sunshine seeped cheer back into the ship. A wisp of a whistle, a snatch of a tune, and Short Davy took to humming.

"Give us a real tune, lad!" Anders shouted from the wheel, "Sing, lad! Sing! I'm sick to dog tired of all this sea-washed moping!"

A grin near split Davy's face. "Yes, sir! A song straightaway, sir!" His foot started tapping the deck boards. "I know just the one." A sweet sound bubbled from his throat and harmony burst into the sunshine.

From the Outer Islands
we sailors do hail.

Chase the wind easterly,
good weather prevails.

The crew let out a shout and joined in for the chorus.

We chase the wind easterly,
good weather prevails.

Davy gave a whoop and continued, the deck crew singing with him in a rousing cacophony of off-key revelry.

Farewell to the farmland
of that we want none.
We're rovers and rogues
'til our sea days be done.

And chase the wind easterly,
good weather prevails.

On waves and through storm,
over deck boards we tread.
We sail those dark seas.
Ain't nothing we dread!

And chase the wind easterly,
good weather prevails.

And chase the wind easterly,
good weather prevails.

The voices soared on the wind, racing upward towards the clouds. For an incandescent instant, the world seemed perfect, melded with camaraderie and harmony. For a moment, the impending trouble washed away in a song. But only for a moment.

For the clock ticked past, and the sky rent in a flash of radiance like lightning though no black clouds threatened and no storm hovered on the horizon. Every voice on the *Jewel* silenced. The wind stilled and the sails lost their billow. The speed of the ship slowed, and every man felt the terrible hush. Another flash of light—not sunlight nor squall, but white incandescence—washed over the ship's bow. Then the silver shadow of the moon crossed the dappled clouds. A screech, born of the deepest darkest torment, shook sea, sky, and ship before all fell silent once more.

Rafe's rushing footsteps broke the quiet as he dashed out onto the deck. A further scream splintered across the sky and seas, and Rafe skidded to a stop.

"I've come for you, brother! Come to make you pay at last!"

An explosion of frosted pale spread from the sky and she appeared, floating against the clouds just beyond the vessel. The Goddess of the Moon shrieked with a burst of prickly laughter, spreading her arms wide above her head, and tossing her unkempt mane of silver hair. On her arm, scratched runes pulsed a deep red.

"My time has come, oh brother! Face me, or I will destroy everything in this world starting with your precious ship!"

Rafe snarled and, in a glow of resplendent blue, leapt into the air. He shot upward on a streak of energy to confront his sister. He skidded to a stop among wisps of airy vapour, hovering a few feet from her, matching her anger face to face.

"Why are you here? Why now? Haven't you done enough? Go back to your island, sister!"

The Goddess of the Moon bowed her head. She uttered her next words in crisp, clear tones. "No, brother. I have not done enough. Never enough! Until you are dead, dead, dead!"

She lifted her head, her eyes burning with a white-hot glow, and a tremendous force of energy swelled from within her entire essence. In the space of a whisper and a heartbeat, she propelled that force directly at Rafe.

Taken unawares, Rafe did little to defend himself and the power hit him full on, smashing him across the sky and driving him down into the sea. The water swallowed him, waves crashing in his wake, and the dark cold pulling him farther into its deep embrace. Through the watery expanse, he could hear the cry of monsters.

Small fractions of panic, and then, swimming frantically up towards the sun, he ascended—fighting the taste of salt, the icy wet, darting fish, and the always, ever-booming scream of beasts—until he broke the surface, gasping pure air and a growing rage. Around him the seas boiled blue as he summoned his power, rising on a tide of magic straight at his sister.

Like a flaming arrow, he careened into her as she countered with a defensive wall of her own power. The impact resounded akin to a ship colliding into submerged rocks and sent them both spinning through the sky. The air shivered with the boom and snapping echo of impacting energy.

On the trailing spirals of magic, Rafe halted his skidding trajectory and scanned the sky for his sister. She laughed and swooped among the clouds, little affected by their skirmish. He took a breath, tasting the copper tang of blood in his mouth. A shiver vibrated along his bones. She was stronger than she should be, stronger than the magic her moon powers granted her. The unsettling thought that she played with him sprung into his mind.

He edged closer, his voice launching questions across the divide that separated them. "Who have you aligned with, sister? What malignant entity augments your power?"

More laughter trilled across the vaporous clouds.

"Caw, caw. Birdie blight.
Feathers black, dark as night.
Oldest born, full of scorn,
Your fate forlorn."

She spun left and dashed forward on a conduit of alabaster moon magic, closing the gap between the two. "Silly brother. Birdie pulls the strings, but I'm the one who stings." She flung her arms up—red runes pounding on her skin—and screamed. A deep guttural yowl that made the wind weep and the air revolve in a whirlwind.

The twisting tempests battered Rafe, tossing him like a toy ship lost at sea, and the rains pummelled him from above. He mustered forth blazing threads of magic and struck back against the storms to break free into clearer sky. He inhaled, and a hand grasped his shoulder. The grinning face of his sister stared at Rafe.

"Time to pay, brother, for your sins."

With a smile, she continually poured every scrap of moon magic and the power of the runes into Rafe.

His scream shattered the surrounding clouds, their vapour dissolving like morning mist in the noonday sun, and the air trembled as repeated shrieks of torment ripped from his throat. Cascades of sparks lit up the empyrean firmament in god-born irradiation, the power of the Moon Goddess grinding its way into Rafe's body. Bone shuddered, muscles jerked in spasms, and his blood sizzled with the influx of her magic.

Maniac laughter gushed from the Goddess of the Moon, chasing her dominion over her brother as she roasted and tortured him. "Die, die, die! No more brother! No more brother!" Power beyond the scope of the gods gushed from her madness, the runes on her arms pulsing a vivid, gleaming crimson. In the cacophony of cackling and sizzling flesh, she never heard the whoosh of the harpoon fired from the *Celestial Jewel*.

The iron and wood projectile pierced the cocoon of magic surrounding both gods and ruptured into an exploding ball of flame. It did little damage to either being but served as distraction enough to halt the Goddess' barrage of death against her brother. Unfortunately, without his sister's magic or his own, Rafe descended from the sky, falling like a stone in a pond.

Screams and cries rose up from the *Jewel*, and an anguished shriek of 'Captain!' followed by the blistering laugh of the Moon Goddess.

Rafe heard it all.

His mind fluttering with unconsciousness, his body wracked with pain, he still ripped a tiny hint of magic from his blood and cushioned his descent, spinning errantly towards his ship. He slammed into the side of the vessel, fingers clutching the rail in a life-saving grip.

Bleeding and broken and clinging to the rail, Rafe stared up at his sister, now readying to attack the ship.

With his last scrap of voice, hoarse and shrill, Rafe screamed a desperate command. "Ring the damn bell!"

Rafe heard running footsteps and the clang of the bell as hands reached over the side and hauled him back on board ship. Above him, his sister screamed. He rolled on his back, his body alive with pain, and looked up.

The sight terrified him.

The Goddess of the Moon gyrated and shuddered against the power of the bell, but held her own against its magic.

"Impossible." A whisper carried on desperation to the clouds. The Goddess of the Moon smiled.

"No, little brother. No. Never impossible. Black wings, magic sings." With those words, crackling energy rained down on the *Celestial Jewel.*

In shrieks and chaos, the crew scattered amid the onslaught, magic raking gouges across the deck and sides, smashing into sail and mast. The foremast cracked with a boom, scattering the sailors underneath lest they be caught by plummeting debris. The upper quarter of the shaft toppled with another loud *snap*, taking out the topgallant sail, the port side rail and a chunk of the deck as it fell before finally sinking into the sea.

Rafe watched his ship smoke and sizzle as magic-born lightning spewed down on them. Fire ignited on the broken mast and the bow, billowing black smoke across streaks of silver. Shudders reverberated along the deck mixing with screams and shouting and running feet. Magic rained conflagration, and injured men fell, some not moving in their silence.

A rumble came from below, and Rafe struggled to his knees fearing another attack. Then a wave washed over the *Jewel*, precisely placed, dousing the fires. A waterspout shot into the sky, smacking the Moon Goddess from her victory and sending her back to the sea. The form of a naked woman rose on another wave and jumped nimbly onto the deck.

"Lynna!"

"Aye, brother. I was tracking her beasts and heard your bell. It seems I arrived in a timely fashion."

"Timely indeed." Rafe stumbled to his feet assisted by Blackthorne, who appeared at his side. "We were about done for."

"You're hurt! What happened?"

"Our sister."

"She did this? Impossible! She's not powerful enough to best you. She can't—"

"Those days are gone, Lynna," a chuckling voice echoed from the sea, and a great serpent arose with the Goddess of the Moon on its back. Its veined wings flapped the wind against the ship's sails, and its mother rubbed the ridge on its head. "Stand aside. Let me finish him. I have no quarrel with you."

Lynna stepped back, moving alongside Rafe and

Blackthorne. "We stand together. Do your worst. We will stop you."

Blackthorne drew his sword with an audible hiss, and several of the *Jewel's* sailors followed his example.

"Rafe lifted his chin and added, We all stand together, sister. All together against your madness."

The Goddess of the Moon looked down from atop her towering monster. She scowled at them. Her fingertips sparked with a white glow, and her arms gleamed red. And then...

Nothing.

She and her monster turned away with a screech and headed out to open waters.

Rafe let out a breath he didn't know he was holding in.

Lynna grunted. "That was... disappointing. She didn't even try to fight."

"I know it doesn't make sense." Blackthorne's puzzled voice broke in, and Lynna cast him a look. Blackthorne blushed. "I mean, ma'am, she was trying to kill us all moments ago. Why didn't she try and finish us? With her power and her beasts..." He let the rest trail off, unwilling to voice the implications.

"She could have won." Rafe said the words for his first mate. "So why didn't she attack?"

Lynna shrugged. "She's always been capricious. Even before. Best not to question it. Accept the good fortune. You've always had the most outrageous luck. It's what saved you today." She grinned. "You're lucky I kept my promise to trail her beasts and heard that infernal bell of yours." Lynna shivered. "I hate the sound of that thing. I don't know how you stand it."

"It's an acquired taste, but you're right. It's luck we survived. Not something I can continue to count on. More extreme measures will have to be taken, I think."

"Now doesn't that sound ominous? Not something I wish to stay for." With a laugh, she dashed for the rail and leapt into the depths of the sea.

"Not much for good-byes, is she sir?"

"No Blackthorne, she isn't. But considering she saved us, I'm not one to complain."

"Aye, she did. It was a close call, it was. Only... Now what, sir?"

Rafe looked around, his heart drowning in the broken bones of his ship. "Now we assess the damage, attend to the injured, and slink off to the nearest port."

"We'll be needing to attend to the dead as well." Blackthorne's voice came quiet, gentle. "At least two men fell in battle, though their ghosts remained with us."

"Who?" Rafe tried to keep the pain out of his voice. He didn't succeed. Hurt doubled, thinking they stayed as ghosts because of him and these troubles.

"Salty Eli. Quiet Peter. Peter died at the bell, but kept it ringing as a spirit."

"He's always been a loyal lad. He deserved better. As

did Eli." Rafe sighed. "Poor lads. We'll bury the corpses at sea unless they want otherwise."

"Aye, sir. Orders for the ship?"

Rafe looked up at the jagged wood that used to be the foremast and the dangling rigging. "The only thing to do now is clean up and patch up best we can. Rig new sails and brace the masts, with a temporary spar to replace the damaged one. Then put into port for proper repairs. We'll sort out our troubles on shore then find a way to deal with my sister and her mess." Another sigh. "And hope we survive."

"Aye, Captain." Blackthorne helped the still wobbly Rafe to lean on the nearby mast. "We'll figure it all out, you'll see. We'll win in the end."

Fog and storm clouds assailed the island at the edge of the world. Overhead the moon shone in the twilight, though the sun caressed the lands beyond this rock in the sea. A goddess sat on the beach, making circles in the sand with a bone. She hummed to herself, a sad lullaby she had almost forgotten.

A crow chased by anger and storm clouds flew loops in the sky above her. Wisps of grey followed the bird as it swooped in for a landing beside the Goddess.

"You failed!" The crow's enraged wail shook the treetops.

"You could have destroyed him! Why didn't you destroy him?"

The Moon Goddess didn't look at the creature, merely dropped her bone, and curled into a ball, her face pouting. "I tried. But *she* came. They were too strong."

"No, they weren't! Not even together! He was weak! You could have killed them both if you wanted too!"

Now she looked at the crow, glaring. "Maybe. Maybe I didn't want. No quarrel with her. With Lynna. Didn't want *her* dead."

The crow flapped its wings in a flurry. "She helped him! She's the enemy!"

"No. Not my enemy. Only him."

"Is he? Is he truly? You had chance after chance and he's still breathing! I don't think you want him dead either!"

"I do!" She scrambled on to all fours and shoved a snarling face at the crow's beak. "I do want him dead!"

"Then why didn't you kill him?"

She sat back on her haunches, her head bowed. "I-I'm not certain. It didn't seem... right." She sighed. "They defended him. They always defend him." Her lip trembled. "But never saw before. Not with my eyes. Up close. It felt... different."

The crow tilted its head. Its eyes staring, puncturing her soul like woodworm. "No, it cannot be." The bird hopped up and down, squawking. "You care." It almost spat the words.

"I don't! Take that back!" The Moon Goddess glared.

"No, it's true. Your heart... It's not dead. Not like it was before. Not black and shrivelled. All light extinguished." The crow hopped back as if she was contagious. "There's a glimmer there now." Disgust dripped from its hoarse voice. "You're worthless! Worthless!"

"I am not!" She roared and swung her fist, smashing it against the bird's head. With an outraged, squealing squawk, it rolled along the sand before taking awkward flight. It circled the scowling Moon Goddess, screaming.

"We are done, you and I! Done!"

"I don't need you little bird! I don't need you!" The Moon Goddess waved her fist and kicked at the sand. "Fly away! Be off with you! Take your gifts! Your power! All useless!"

"Bah! You are the useless one! Keep the magic for all the good it will do you! Your brother will come, and you will be weak! You will be weak!"

The Nightmare Crow screeched and flew towards the moon over the sea.

Chapter Fourteen
Consequence

The faint strains of the keening lament reached the ship first as they sailed the battered and ungainly *Jewel* towards the harbour at Black Shoals. From the temple on the hill above the port, rows of priests knelt before the gate. They lined the pathway and entrance garden while wailing entreaties fled from their throats to the heavens. Behind them, a throng of the dead milled about and moaned.

"Well that won't do them one bit of bloody good," muttered One-Eyed Anders as he steered the ship towards port below the Black Shoals Temple.

"It might ease their fear," came the captain's reply.

"Well, it don't ease mine none. That bloody bawling gives me the shivers, it does."

Rafe remained silent secretly agreeing with Anders. The sound grated on his nerves like the hull of a ship scraping on coral. But those were his people. He limped to the rail and forced himself to watch the spectacle.

The welcome did not improve as they came in to drop anchor. Curses and glares from the shore crew met the ship's heaving lines, but the sullen workers helped moor their ship, nonetheless. Jeers followed as the ship finished docking and then the men of the *Jewel* were left to their own company.

Rafe turned to face his crew, his face pale, his eyes full of pain. "Men, I'll be going ashore to report to the harbourmaster and then to visit the temple. Blackthorne, Pinky, Davy you're with me." He gave a slight nod. "The rest of you, clear away any remaining debris and start the minor repairs. I'll attend to the ship's larger needs when I return." Several murmurs shifted across the deck, and a few crew members eyed the captain's still shaky state with uncertainty.

Sensing the unease, he added, "We can't afford to dawdle. We need to be seaworthy as soon as possible." He drew back his shoulders and gave his best stern stare. "You have your orders!" The crew chosen to accompany him flocked to his side, and the rest turned to ship duties. Then the four men went ashore, straight to the office of the harbourmaster.

The door creaked open on neglected hinges, and a stocky man looked up from a worn pine desk as they walked into his workplace. He shuffled aside some papers and frowned. "Well, well, Captain Morrow. Didn't expect to see you again. Not after..." He let the words hang and drummed his fingers on his desk. "If I was you, I'd turn around and sail on out to sea. I don't know what you've done exactly with them portals, but folks been agitated for the past two days."

Rafe replied to his manner softly, "We will stay only as long as necessary. We have some repairs, and I have business at the temple."

The harbourmaster shrugged. "Your affair, I suppose. Consider yourself reported in and make it a short trip."

Rafe nodded, and he and his men left without another word.

Outside, a tall, hard-faced man waited, his foot tapping impatiently. By his uniform and insignia, he held the rank of commander in the Royal Navy of the Seven Kingdoms. He stepped in front of Rafe and his men, blocking the path to pass.

"I thought that was you, Captain Morrow. You've certainly bungled things up this time, haven't you? Turned this whole territory into somewhat of a powder keg. I can tell you, as a representative of the Royal Navy, I'm not very happy with this mess you created."

Rafe bristled as did his men, but he held his composure. He smiled coldly and replied, "And who are you, sir, that I should be concerned of your opinion?" Rafe took satisfaction in the shocked and outraged look that sliced across the commander's face.

"I'm Commander Augustus Quartermain Pelham! Commanding officer of the King's Rock Fort here at Black Shoals! And you, sir, are nothing more than a scallywag captain who needs to answer for your reckless actions!"

"Why you—" Blackthorne's raised voice was cut off a wave by Rafe's hand and a snap of words. "Don't Blackthorne. No need to get into a quarrel on my behalf." He smiled at the commander. "Why indeed, sir, I am a captain, but you forget yourself and your place in the scheme of things." He took a breath and a step closer to the naval officer. "For I am also a god, capable of turning your ordered existence into something far less pleasant." Rafe watched the man's skin turn two shades paler. "So watch your tongue, *sir*. Or I just might cut it out."

"Are you threatening me?"

"Yes." For a second, Rafe's eyes sparked with blue energy.

"Well, I—I don't—it doesn't," The commander stumbled over his words before finally spitting out, "You can lord it over us. Think you've won. Think you're so superior, but you'll answer for this. Opinion's shifted against you, Captain. You'll see, and it's still shifting. You may find even gods fall to earth and have to pay for the things they've done."

The man spun on his heel and trotted off without another word.

"Damnation! This is what I said might happen. Damn navy!" Blackthorne scowled and spat in the dirt.

Behind him, Pinky and Short Davy chuckled. Pinky exclaimed, "The captain put him in his place though, and did it brilliantly."

"Don't laud my efforts, yet. The harbourmaster said much the same thing, remember. It isn't likely people will receive us kindly for a while. Not until we put the world right. Not until we find a way to defeat my sister."

"That's going to be a tall order." Davy gasped as soon as the words left his mouth and hastily added, "But you'll find a way, sir, we all know that. I'm sorry, sir."

"Don't worry about it, Davy. We're all thinking it. She dealt us a blow this time, she did." Rafe gave his man a sad smile. "And we will find a way, but first to business. To the temple, men."

And the four sailors set off.

The temple lay to the northeast of the town, and they skirted the edge of the settlement. The waterfront and adjoining streets seemed quiet, subdued. No laughter or chatter greeted them. No casual foot traffic. No vendors hawking wares or buskers looking for coin. Only faces staring from windows, or people lingering on stoops and open doorways.

And the heavy air of distrust and malignancy.

The townsfolk they saw cast looks of fear and antipathy at the quartet and glared as they walked past. Some slammed themselves behind their doors or snapped shut their curtains in the crew's wake. And, most of all, whispers under the breath dogged their footsteps.

Rafe gritted his teeth. "We get this done and then let us be out of this place."

His companions nodded and they doubled timed their pace to the temple.

As they arrived, they found the gates ajar and the garden path empty. Wails still drifted from the shore, and not a priest came out to greet them. In the mixed air of silence and yowled mourning, they hurried to see the temple spellcaster. Rafe knocked on the door painted a summer sea blue and a faint "enter" echoed out to the men. The captain turned the handle, and they stepped inside a sanctum.

A dark-haired woman sat by the far corner in a high-backed wicker chair behind a round table. She smiled as they entered, the first friendly greeting they encountered since coming ashore.

"Exalted One. How may I be of service to you on this day?"

"Hello, Aylia. I need to send a message to all the temples regarding the portals."

"I thought as much. Dire days these are. I don't envy you your duties or the task ahead of you."

She rose from her chair and walked to the shelves lining the opposite wall. She took down a small, carved wooden box. She then moved to the table, placed the box down, and seated herself back in her chair.

"Shall we begin?" She waved a hand towards Rafe to join her. He pulled over another chair and sat across from her. The rest of the crew remained standing near the door. Aylia unfastened the box and removed three spellcaster crystals, arranging them in a triangular shape.

She glanced at Rafe. "What message, and where do you want it sent?"

"Send it to all the Soul Temples in the Outer Islands and the Seven Kingdoms. Tell them I was the one who closed the portals to protect the After World from invasion by the Goddess of the Moon and her sea beasts. The balance will be restored when she is defeated." Aylia reacted with a slight intake of breath. Rafe paused for a moment and then continued, "And I'll need another message sent to the Oracle as well. Tell her, 'Expect the *Celestial Jewel* in Blue Bay port. I need to speak with her.'"

Aylia nodded, summoned her magic, and activated the spellcaster crystals. She intoned Rafe's messages, and they watched the stones radiate and the words scrawl into the air. Shapes and letters materialized into green light—dozens of missives bound for the temples—before being transmitted along the caster's ethereal network.

"There. The messages are sent, waiting in the stones to be read by my fellows. I hope this will alleviate some of the fears and uncertainty of late."

"I hope so as well." Rafe pushed out his chair and

rose to leave, but Aylia laid a hand on his arm.

"Will she be defeated?" A soft whisper, but it reached Rafe's ears.

For a moment he thought to lie, yet answered, "I don't know, but I will try."

Aylia removed her hand with a sigh. "That's all we can ask of you, Exalted One."

He nodded, oddly comforted. Then he and his men took their leave.

On the return trip, they again strolled empty paths until they neared the harbour. They heard the yelling first, a hullaballoo of angered voices. Then, as they restlessly rounded a corner, a group of unruly townspeople and deceased spirits surged to accost Rafe. Bodies and lingering souls surrounded him, pushing and clawing at his person, and a chorus of questions bombarded him as a rushing tide.

"What happened?"

"Why can't the remaining dead cross?"

"Why has the portal closed?"

"Has the After World been destroyed?"

The deluge of voices hit the captain square, but it was the defeated howl of the dead that broke him.

"Enough! I've had enough! What do you expect from me? I did what had to be done to save us all, living and dead!"

Silence dropped like an anchor and the crowd

stumbled back in shock and fear. Rafe glared at the throng, waiting for the first man to challenge him. But the challenge came from behind.

"Sir." The calm voice of Blackthorne broke the silence.

Rafe whirled, his expression a fearsome thing. "What do *you* want!?" He barked at his first mate, the words as sharp as any blade.

Blackthorne retreated a step but persisted in his duty. "Sir. You are glowing."

That set Rafe back a peg. "Excuse me?"

"You are glowing. A rather nice shade of pale blue. But it may be a bit intimidating to those unaccustomed." He nodded at the now cowering crowd.

Rafe glanced at himself. He had unconsciously manifested his power in his anger. He gazed at the gathered people. Looks of terror, bewilderment, awe, and astonishment peppered their faces.

It would be so easy to sweep them aside. One flick of my hand and they would tumble like summer waves.

Rafe sighed. He allowed the light and his magic to fade. Instead, he shouted, "Let us pass!"

The assembled grumbled and whined, but not a man nor spirit stood in Rafe's way. He and the crew advanced unchallenged and returned to their ship. The sight of the *Jewel's* broken mast and rail and her other damage, did nothing to alleviate Rafe's mood as they boarded. There was work to be done.

"Listen up, men! Time to repair this ship and sail out of this port! Most of you know what's coming. For the rest, clear the deck and stay out of my way!"

Rafe watched the crew scurry below. Blackthorne, casting him a worried look, waited until he was alone on deck. Then he sat crossed-legged on the boards, placing his palms against the wood. He let the ship's magic flow into him, feeling the wounds.

He whispered, "I know you're hurting. I'm here. We'll get you fixed up."

He called forth his own energy, sending it into the ship, strengthening the vessel, uniting with the power that coursed through the ship. Their combined force streamed into the ruined areas, rebuilding, mending the broken. The mast and rail knitted themselves whole, the scorch marks vanished, shattered wood, gouges, scars all healed and faded, transforming the parts into something strong and new. At the end, Rafe slouched in near exhaustion, vitality ebbing, but the *Jewel* restored to seaworthy.

"That's better now, isn't it." Rafe managed a smile as footsteps sounded on deck. As usual, Blackthorne reached his side first.

"Are you all right, Captain?"

"Yes. Just tired. But the ship's repaired. We can continue." He raised a hand. "Help me up."

Blackthorne aided the captain to his feet. "I'll assist you to your cabin, sir."

"Not yet. I'll see us out first." He nodded at a crate by the forecastle. "That will do for a seat until we're out of port." Blackthorne assisted him and let him ease onto the crate, leaning against the comfort of his ship.

Across the deck, the helmsman cried out, "Call the course, Captain!"

For a flicker of time, he thought of sailing past open waters into the unknown, leaving it all behind. Then he gave the order, "Set the heading to Rock Island Temple. Time to consult the Oracle, boys." And the ship set sail manoeuvring out of dock and past the harbour until Black Shoals retreated in its rear view.

Rafe sighed.

At least the Oracle will welcome us. This one will be a simple stop.

Chapter Fifteen
Rock Island Temple

The following morning, neither sound nor sign of life wafted out of the harbour as the *Jewel* sailed into the cove at Rock Island. They were the only outside ship in the Blue Bay port, and an air of hushed morbidity settled along the sea and win. The reverberating slap of waves against docks and the hiss of the wind enhanced the feeling of emptiness. A prickle ratcheted its way along Rafe's spine echoed by the soft nervous whispers snaking through the ship's crew.

One-Eyed Anders gave voice to their unease. "Where is everyone? Do you think they were attacked?"

"Perhaps they've just gone inland for protection." Rafe tried to make his voice sound confident, but he didn't believe his words. Too much had happened.

"And not leave a crew to man the harbour, to help dock the ships coming in? It don't feel right."

"I know." The whisper slipped out despite the captain's best intentions. "Take her into dock, Anders. We'll land a few men, and then you take her out again. Wait offshore until we return." Rafe strode to the helm and gave the wheel a feather touch of magic and whispered words. "She'll take you in now. Just steer her gently."

"Aye, Captain. I'll guide her true and tender."

Anders made to steer the ship into anchor straight as a cannon shot, though, in truth, the ship took herself in with little help from its helmsman. Rafe stood on deck as they docked, but could see nary a soul and no one came to greet them as the ship berthed.

"Short Davy, Striker Angus, Pinky Jasper. You three are with me. Blackthorne, you have the ship."

"But, sir—"

"Not this time, Blackthorne. I need you here with the ship." Rafe turned and gave him a hard look, something he knew his first mate would understand. "Something about this feels... atypical. I don't think this is my sister's doing. In case something goes awry, I need you here. I'm counting on you."

Blackthorne straightened his spine. "Aye, Captain."

"Good man." He gave them all a smile. "We'll get to the bottom of this. All right you three. Let's go ashore."

The captain and his men disembarked and stood on the dock for a moment as the *Jewel* sailed out of the harbour and back out to more open waters. Then the others looked to Rafe for orders.

"To the harbourmaster's first. See if there's anybody at home."

Not a soul, living or dead, met them as they made their way to the familiar building and entered. Inside, more silence and sunlight peering through the half-open window greeted them. A gust of wind slipped through and rattled the bones of a warding ornament hanging from the ceiling. A few papers littered the floor.

"It ain't like the harbourmaster to leave the place unmanned, and I ain't never seen harbour records on the floor like that." Pinky chattered to fill the quiet. "He likes everything in its place."

Rafe bent down and scooped up the documents, glancing at them. He saw a manifest and docking records for the ship, *Black Bastion*.

"I know this ship. From Crickwell Island. It's captained by Eva Erickson."

"Sir?" The puzzled voice of Short Davy broke through his musings.

"These papers." Rafe waved the records in his hand. "They belong to the *Black Bastion*. You remember. She survived the last moon storm, came into port as we left that night. She does supply runs between this port, Crickwell Island, Tenby Key, and Black Shoals. If her papers are out, then chances are she docked recently." A tingle, a strange sensation of trepidation, stirred in Rafe's blood like something out of place and waiting.

"She ain't in the harbour, so she must've headed back out. Probably took the long route 'round the seaward side of the island. Going towards Tenby or Black Shoals maybe. We would have seen or met her, otherwise." Angus tossed his opinion into the mix.

"Unless the ship never left the island." The captain's words tumbled out, almost of their own accord.

"But she's not in port," protested Angus.

"The Old North Harbour, you mean?" Pinky cottoned to Rafe's thought. "Yah, we could've missed her, if she's anchored there."

"But why?" Short Davy chimed in.

Rafe sighed, having little in the way of answer save the unease in his blood. "Whatever the reason, if they are there, it bears ill will, I think."

"Do we head back, signal the ship, and check out the Old North Harbour?" Striker Angus seemed eager at this prospect.

"Sorry to disappoint you, Mr. Angus, but no. We press on to the Temple." The disquiet fairly snapped at his nerves at the mention of it. "I want to check on the Oracle."

There were silent nods of ascent, and the group left the harbourmaster to wind their way through town. The same empty, calm foreboding pervaded the streets. Not a person, not a laugh, no footsteps, no whispers surrounded them. Simply the swish of ocean waves, the rustle of breeze, and the lonely cry of seabirds.

"Where are all the people?" Short Davy hissed his worry out loud. "Where did they all go? The last time we were here—"

"Aye." Angus clapped him on the shoulder in an attempt to reassure. "I know. 'Tis most peculiar."

"It's malfeasance, that's what is! Sinister doings!" Pinky clenched his hands into fists and shivered under his skin.

"Good thing Mouse isn't here. The poor boy would have a fit." Short Davy smiled, despite everything.

Angus and Pinky both snorted with Pinky exclaiming, "The boy would faint dead away more like."

Rafe listened to the banter, glad the crew had ceased to question him. The closer they got to the Rock Island Temple, the stronger his premonition of dread became. He knew they were headed for trouble, but he didn't know why or what.

Perhaps it was the strange lack of human sound. Even on the climb to the temple, only the noise of nature enveloped them. Screeching seabirds and twittering songbirds, the rustle of underbrush from fleeing marmots, the flutter of leaves in the wind, and the ever-present sound of the ocean. But not the slightest peep of a human voice, a clang of a hammer, a creak of a wheel, or any footstep save their own.

"Do you think everyone just sailed away? Got on ships and left?" Short Davy kept on with his questions.

Pinky sniffed. "It'd be odd if they did. And why not

use their own fishing vessels? They're seaworthy enough. Get them to another island at least. I mean, if they were evacuating or something."

"You're right, that would be odd." Rafe suddenly spoke up. "But they may have evacuated all the same. There's an inland settlement."

"I remember hearing about that. Old Town they call it now, don't they?"

"Yes. It used to be the hub of this place, until Blue Bay and the temple was built for the Oracle. The place even had a road leading to landing docks for ships. Then everyone migrated to the new port, and the place all but died out."

Pinky nodded. "That makes sense. With the attacks, people moved out of harm's way. For the time being."

But Rafe was not convinced, and his apprehension slipped out. "It doesn't explain why there was no harbourmaster or no sounds from the temple. We're close enough to hear voices or singing."

"No, it doesn't." Pinky frowned, any relief draining from his face. The others captured similar looks.

After that, no one voiced any question or said another word. They arrived at the temple gates in silence.

The entrance was slightly ajar as they approached. The group ignored the bell and pushed through to an empty courtyard. Not a soul hurried out to greet them. They could see that main hall doors were, like the gates, partially open.

Rafe's skin shivered at the sight of it. He nodded towards the hall. "That's where we'll be needing to go, boys. For good or ill."

The three crewmen chorused, "Aye, sir."

The men walked into the grand hall, their boots clacking on the marble floor. The room was dimly lit by sunlight flickering through a line of windows, but they could see chairs, sculptures, and people.

"Glad you could finally join us, Captain Morrow."

Eva Erikson, the captain of the *Black Bastion*, stood in the middle of the hall, sword drawn at the ready. Scattered around the hall were many of her crew, and some of the temple acolytes, bound and gagged. To Erikson's left, the Oracle knelt on the grey marble floor, head lowered.

"Do you like my welcome, Captain Morrow?" Erikson smiled. "I prepared it especially for you. Dressed all your pretty dolls up right." She laughed. "Your temple and all your precious half-wit believers are in my control now. As are you!"

Fury and magic stirred in his blood, but Rafe kept his calm, as—he was proud to see—did his crew. Nerves twitching, he said with a touch of mockery, "Quite an accomplishment, Captain Erikson, taking the temple. Few would dare, let alone succeed."

"You would think so. Not that it matters. I'm in charge now."

"Still. I wonder how you accomplished it? Was it just luck?"

"Luck! What arrogant drivel! It was my plan that did it! I outsmarted you, and your people!"

Rafe repressed a retort. She was still as arrogant as ever. He took a deep breath and continued to engage her. "So how did it happen? Exactly?"

"Now wouldn't you like to know, but I'll keep mum for now." She took a step forward. "Have your lot on their knees, and no surprises."

Striker Angus bristled. "Say the word, Captain, and we'll rush 'em. We can take this rabble."

"I'm sure you can, but people might get hurt. Do as she says, for now."

His men knelt as bid, though Captain Erikson scowled. "Your crew is as bloody arrogant as you! I'm in control! They need to do as I say!"

"Of course you are." Rafe's voice came at her as calm as a sunny day at sea. "You're in charge. But I would like to know what you did with the townsfolk? Where are the people of Blue Bay?"

"Oh, so now you have concern for the common folk, do ya? Well, I ain't going to tell ya!"

"Did you kill them?"

"Did I... why you—"

"They're safe!" The Oracle shouted, interrupting Captain Erikson. "They're in Old Town!"

"Shut up!" Erikson backhanded her, making her mouth bleed at the corner. "Or better yet, why not tell him about your complicity. How you helped me lay this trap."

The Oracle remained silent.

"Not talking? Don't blame you. Did you know she and the port made this practical evacuation plan? Ship 'em all out of Blue Bay to Old Town if there was an attack? Ever the dutiful servant, her." Erikson sneered. "When we arrived last night, I brought word of approaching sea creatures. Lied of course, but it got the port deserted enough. In a couple of hours, all's left were the harbourmaster and a few of his men. Easy as scraping barnacles to round them up and use as hostages to open the temple gates."

"You threatened to kill those people!" The Oracle snapped, her eyes dancing daggers at her captor.

"The threat worked didn't it?" Erikson laughed and scoffed at Rafe. "She even helped me keep the Blue Bay folk down in Old Town settlement. Told them to stay put this morning and not return. Still too dangerous, she said. You should have seen her, messaging them by spellcaster. Selling a tall tale of creatures sighted off the coast. Put the fear of the damned into them, she did. You would have been proud of her, I suspect." Erikson smiled. "Why, she's even the reason we knew you was coming. Told us to expect you today."

Rafe glanced at Amaratha, who stared at the marble floor.

"Ah, disappointed in your little pet. You should be. It's her that let me set up this scene for you. I sent up spotters to the ridge after she revealed your imminent arrival and the minute they spied your ship coming I set up my greeting."

"Well, aren't you the clever one." The sarcasm slipped out at the sight of Erikson's smug expression.

"Yeah, I am." Erikson spat. "Clever enough to have you at my mercy. Now you have to do what you're told, for a change. Have someone in charge of your life instead of the other way 'round."

Rafe flexed his fingers, trying hard not to hit the woman. Instead, he asked, "Well then, you have me here. What is this all about? What do you want?"

She glared. "It's about living in fear. Every damned moonrise, waiting on the storms, on those beasts. I lost four men last storm, and two the moonrise before that. And now... now they're coming whenever, hitting towns, killing..." Her voice cracked, and her jaw clenched. "And now you're closing off portals, scaring folks. You're a damnable menace."

"I know the portals sealing was traumatic, but—"

"Shut up!" She shouted down Rafe's attempted explanation. "I don't want your excuses! I want you to fix this! To do something! Make all the bloody sea creatures go back to their dark pits and leave us all be! Fight that damn Goddess of the Moon!"

That surprised him, and his control slipped. He snapped back, "What do you think I've been doing?"

Erikson snarled. "Bloody nothing, that's what! This ain't going to be solved by sailing about with warnings and soothing feelings! You need to take action! You need to fight! Or do you just like lording it over the rest of us? Prancing about as if you were better than everyone? If you're so much in charge, then put it all right. Now!" Her voice snapped in bitterness and frustration. "You're a menace. Hoodwinking the innocent into believing your lies. You probably started all this." Captain Erikson shot daggers at him with her stare. "My sister was a priestess at Star Reef Temple and now she's gone." She moved her hand to the hilt of her sword. "Can you bring her back? Can you?"

Rafe hissed in a breath and released it into the thick tension. "No. Nothing can bring her back."

"I know. But it's your fault. And you're going to make it right. And here's why." Erikson reached over and grabbed the Oracle by the arm, pulling her to her feet. She pushed Amaratha in front of Rafe.

"She's yours, right? The precious Oracle with all the visions! All the answers?"

Rafe nodded. An uneasy sensation crept into his bones. "She can't help you. Let her go." He extended a hand, but Erikson yanked Amaratha out of reach.

"Now, now. Don't touch." Captain Erikson released

the Oracle and took a step back. "I'm not asking her to help. She's the one who's going to pay your toll."

Amaratha turned half a step, obscuring Rafe's view. Her voice echoed through the room, "What are you doing? How do you expect—" Her words broke off with a choking noise, and a sucking squish. A rasping hiss followed from the Oracle's throat, and her body twisted. Then Rafe saw. Blood covered the front of Amaratha's dress and Erickson's sword was stabbed into her gut.

"Paid in full, Captain Morrow" Captain Erikson smiled and withdrew her blade from the Oracle's belly. Small drops from the weapon fell in red stains upon the marble.

The Oracle collapsed to her knees, clutching her abdomen. For a moment, she looked at the God of Souls sadness etched on her face. Then Amaratha's eyes glazed in the frost of death and Rafe watched her life drain to its last breath. Her body fell to the floor and blood slowly seeped across the marble.

Then a shimmer shadowed the body that rippled against flesh and the surrounding air. Time slowed, tick by tick, with every mortal breath becoming endless in length. Only Rafe stood unchanged as he watched death unfold its last phenomenon. He shoved away his dread and sorrow and waited. Gently, the Oracle's spirit rose from her corpse and drifted to him.

"Don't blame yourself for this. I know you'll try, but

don't." She smiled, words gliding softly to his ears alone. "Death comes to us all, and it simply is our time to say goodbye, Captain Morrow." She sighed, a little regret mixed with affection. "I can feel the After World calling to me. I can't linger long lest I remain bound here. I just have one last message for you." Her ghostly hand stroked his cheek. "Face the past. Go home to the gods. Tell them that war has come. Your father holds the key." And with a smile she faded from this world, breaking another corner off Rafe's heart.

"That was payment for my sister." A voice jolted the captain back to the world of the living. He stared into the smirking face of Captain Erikson. She took a step forward, her sword trailing drops of blood.

"Now, you will open the portals and destroy those sea creatures! Or she'll be just the first one of these foolish followers to die!"

Rafe glared at Captain Erikson with a stare colder than the bottomless depths of the sea and harder than the bloodied steel in her hand.

"No."

He spoke one word, but it sent a shiver deep into the bone of all present. "However," Rafe summoned the magic from the quintessence of his being and shone with a dark sapphire radiance. "Someone else will die. You."

The light bolted free in snaking tentacles, stabbing Captain Erikson through the throat and chest. She didn't scream. She didn't bleed. She went stiff and pale. Gurgling whimpers emanated from her throat. The sword dropped from her hand, clanging onto the marble floor. Not one person rushed to her aid. They all seemed mesmerized.

Then Rafe ripped out her soul.

Erikson's spirit stood, open-mouthed, and watched her body crumble to the floor beside the Oracle's corpse. Rafe smiled at her. "Welcome to the world of the spirits, Captain Erikson. Enjoy your stay. It will be a long one."

Chapter Sixteen
Riptide

Shock shattered across the hall with the eyes of every person fixed on the body of Captain Erikson and the manifestation of Rafe's godly form. Erikson's ghost collapsed, shrieking. Rafe chuckled, and the temple acolytes winced.

He then turned on the rest of his adversaries. "This is what I can do to all fools who challenge me!"

His words ruptured the disbelief, and one of the crewmen of the *Black Bastion* charged forward, his sword halfway out of its sheath. Rafe flicked his wrist, and the man immobilized in mid-attack. Rafe slithered a tendril of light outward and pierced the man's chest. He drew the man's soul out slowly, letting him gasp for breath. Another sword fell with a clang, the fingers holding it, now useless.

With a smile, Rafe withdrew his magic. The man fell to his knees, soul intact, and sobbing. He crawled away, the fight in him vanished. The rest of the assembled crew took a step back.

Rafe took a breath, letting his anger flow. The sapphire colour surrounding him deepened, adjusting to indigo. "The crew of the *Black Bastion* will leave this place! You will crawl back to your ship and slink away like the treacherous curs you have proven yourselves to be! You will spread the word of your Captain's fate! Let the islands know what happens when you cross me!"

Faces blanched, but not a soul moved. One brave man ventured a question. "What about Captain Erikson's body?"

"It stays here! No one touches the murderer!" Rafe took a step forward and bellowed, "Go now! Leave this place before I change my mind and you share your captain's fate!"

Terrified sailors scattered, fleeing the captain's wrath and abandoning plans and erstwhile hostages. The echo of running footstep and the jeers of Rafe's crew bounced off the walls.

Erikson's ghost screamed, "Don't you abandon me!" She spirited forward after her men. Rafe closed his fingers into a fist and yanked her tethered spirit to a halt. Another jerk and she tumbled along the floor. She gazed into the fury of Rafe's eyes and crawled into a corner. She huddled, arms wrapped around her knees and loudly wept, her cries crashing through the hall.

Rafe released a breath and let his magic slowly fade.

"Men, get those acolytes free of their bonds."

The crew hesitated, and then Short Davy addressed his captain, "Gladly, sir, but those men… they're escaping. We need to warn the *Jewel*, get—"

"I gave an order! Now get to it!"

His startled crew hopped to obey, slicing ropes that bound hands and untying gags. Rafe found a cloth and covered the Oracle. Her congealing blood seeped into the white fabric. Then he looked up to see his crew gathered before him, hands on hips with rather distressed expressions.

Rafe sighed. "Something wrong, boys?"

"By the bones, there is! I can't believe you're just letting those scallywags go!" An aggrieved Pinky snapped the question into the air, breaking the tension. "They need to pay! Just like that piece of bilge water caterwauling in the corner." He flipped his head at Captain Erikson. "And speaking of her, can you get her to shut up? Her wailing is hurting my ears."

"I can obligate you on that front." With an amused smirk, Rafe summoned a touch of magic, and nothing but silence came from Erikson's throat. She buried her head in her hands and cried harder. Tears with no sound.

Rafe looked at his crew, their waiting faces still upset. They did deserve an explanation. "I know you don't like it, but, yes. I am letting those men go free." A hiss, a gasp, and a "bloody hell" tumbled from the crew's lips.

Rafe squared his shoulders and continued. "I do this

because I want them to spread the story of what happened here. I want people to know what I did. To make them remember who I truly am. Something like this cannot happen again. Especially not now." He glanced down at the Oracle's shrouded body. "I think I've been hiding behind my facade too long."

"So the God of Souls will show his true face to the world?"

A tiny feminine voice joined the conversion. A petite dark-haired priestess stepped forward. She stared at Rafe with awe and expectation, rubbing her wrists.

Rafe gently smiled at her. "I think, for a little while at least, he will. What's your name, child?"

"Rayla. I'm a senior priestess here."

"Good. You can help me then. We still have things to put right." He swung on his crew, who now appeared slightly more mollified. "You too, boys. There's still work to finish. Angus. Hightail on down to the port and signal the *Jewel*. Get her headed back into the harbour. Short Davy, find the spellcaster and send a message to Old Town. Tell the folk what's happened and that it's safe to return to Blue Bay if they wish."

He glanced at Rayla. "As to that, where are the harbourmaster and his men? And the remaining acolytes. I know the temple housed more people. Were they killed?"

"No. Tied up and locked in the wine cellars. That one," She shot hatred at the blubbering remains of

Erikson, "wanted only manageable numbers in the hall."

"That's a blessing, at least. Pinky, take a few priests and go free them. We'll need shore crew to dock the *Jewel*."

"Aye, Captain." He hurried off, joining the crew already at work at their assigned tasks.

Rafe gave Rayla a strange look. "That only leaves the bodies."

"Yes." Unspoken grief for the Oracle and mutual loathing for her killer hung between them. "We will prepare the Oracle's body and see to her burial. The temple has its own graveyard. I would ask you to stay, but I suspect you have more pressing matters."

"I do." He sadly smiled, wanting to stay. "And what of this?" He prodded Erikson's corpse with his foot.

"I say toss her off the cliff into the sea."

The ghost abruptly jumped to her feet and silently screamed, unvoiced anguish streaming out in a pitiful, soundless plea.

"Apparently, she's not in favour of this plan." Rafe raised his hand and triggered his magic. He glared at Erikson. "I'll let you speak. But no screams, and no weeping." He gestured his fingers.

The words poured out of the ghost. "Please don't. Please. Don't toss me into the sea. Send my body back to my family or bury me here on the island. Don't condemn my remains to the cold depths."

Rayla sneered. "That almost sounds like you're afraid."

"She probably is. Many sailors dread being buried at sea. Being lost forever under the waves with the ghouls and the monsters. It's almost tempting to do it."

Erikson went pale, even for a spirit. "Please, no. You know the stories. What can happen to sailors' bodies..." Her spirit shuddered. Her voice, begging. "You know there are things worse than monsters waiting under the sea. Whatever I've done, don't condemn me to that."

Rafe tilted his head. "I didn't take you for the superstitious kind, but you may be right. Dark things are stirring. It's not the time for vengeance, and, whatever you believe of me, I'm not cruel." He laid a hand on Rayla's shoulder. "Do you think you have it in you to preserve the body and send it home to her family?"

"I suppose. They probably deserve that mercy, even if she doesn't."

The ghost sunk back to the floor, relief on her face.

"At least she's quieted." Rayla smirked. "Which reminds me, if you will permit the question, Exalted One, how did your crew hear her earlier? I thought only your acolytes had that gift?"

"Serve on my ship long enough, and the magic seeps into your bones. This world and the next start to merge."

"If they are even separate to begin with."

"What?" Her words nudged a memory in Rafe's brain. A voice he heard a long time ago.

"Something the Oracle said to me. That the world of

the living and the word of spirit are not apart, not separate. Not two places, but halves of one whole. The thought stayed with me. That we are all, living and dead, connected."

"It sounds like something she'd say. Beautiful and cryptic." Rafe smiled, if only briefly. "Speaking of which, we need to honour her remains. Shall we?"

Rayla nodded and together, along with a few others, they removed the bodies from the hall, one set for preservation and the other taken to be prepared for burial. When the pair returned to the hall they found an outraged harbourmaster complaining and waiting with his men and Rafe's crew.

Rafe staved off any outbursts by barking orders. "Angus! Report! Did the *Jewel* head to port?"

"Aye, sir! Took the liberty of borrowing a bit of signal magic from the dockside, sir, and sent a message. The ship's headed back."

"Good man. Now be so kind as to escort the harbourmaster and his men back. I expect he'd like to put things shipshape with his office and ready a place for my ship."

"Indeed, I would! And have a sharp word with Captain Erikson! Where is that bounder?"

A moan from her ghost heralded Rafe's question, "You didn't tell him?"

"We tried sir," Short Davy sounded both frustrated and apologetic. "He wouldn't let us get a word in edgewise. This is the quietest—"

The harbourmaster interrupted. "Tell me what?"

"Captain Erikson is dead." Rafe had the slight satisfaction of seeing the man blanch. "And her crew sent sailing. You won't get any more trouble from them. I guarantee it."

"Oh." The man composed himself quickly. "That's good then. Back to port. Come along men." He whirled about and strode from the temple, his bewildered men following him.

"Go with him, Angus, and wait for the *Jewel*. We'll be along shortly."

With a grin, Striker Angus raced to catch up with the harbourmaster.

Rafe turned back to Short Davy and Pinky. "The message got off to Old Town? The rest of the acolytes are all right?"

The pair answered in turn, Davy speaking first. "Yes, sir. I spoke to Old Town. The Council was upset to hear what happened, and they'll be sending people back to Blue Bay." He turned to Rayla. "And to help here at the Temple, ma'am." Rayla nodded her thanks.

"A couple of your people are a bit shook," Pinky added, "but they're being tended to. The rest insisted to go about their duties. Even after I told them the sad news. They're a fine lot. You should be proud."

Rayla smiled, and Pinky blushed, revealing the reason for his nickname.

Amused, but sympathetic, Rafe ended Pinky's discomfort. "You two wait for me outside. I have one last bit of business and then we'll remove ourselves to the port before Blackthorne storms the place."

With snickers and an, "Aye, sir," they ambled from the temple hall.

Rayla's soft voice broke the sudden quiet. "What business remains?"

"A hard question. I dislike asking this so soon, but do you have a successor to the Oracle?"

Rayla sighed. "A hard question, indeed, but one the needs asking." She stared at the red blood stains on the marble floor. "The times give us no leeway to mourn, do they?"

"No." Sensing her hesitation, he pressed. "So, is there a successor?"

This time she did not hedge her answer. "Yes. The new Oracle lives on Tenby Key. We will fetch her as soon as possible."

"Good. How old is she?"

"She is fifteen. Young, but strong."

"Not ideal, but it could be worse." He now glanced at the blood stain. "Amaratha came here when she was but six years."

"Yes. But she adjusted well to her new life. She is a great loss to us all. Especially at this time."

"Yes. She will be missed." A shadow of sadness passed over Rafe's face. "I wish I could stay, but..." His words trailed off with a hint of regret and discomfiture.

"Yes, I know. The God of Souls is needed elsewhere."

"Yes, I—" He paused abruptly, her words triggering the memory of a forgotten task in Rafe's mind. "There is one more thing. You're owed an explanation regarding the portals. I—"

"No need to explain." Rayla interrupted with a smile. "We are aware of what happened with the Kraken, and what you did to protect the After World. As well as the unexpected battle with your sister. Such things reverberate with the Oracle." She quirked the edge of her mouth. "You should know that."

"I should. Farewell, then. I'll return when I can."

As he turned to leave, he heard Erikson's voice. "What about me? Where am I to go? How do I pass to the After World?"

Rafe faced her ghost down. "You don't go anywhere. Any soul taken by me is marked. There will be no After World for you until I choose to let you pass. Your spirit will remain in this temple doing penance for your crime. Pray the sisters don't decide to toss you in the sea to be eaten."

Rafe spun on his heel and left, the satisfying echo of her screams ushering him out, followed by Rayla's laughter. Outside, he joined his crew, who were waiting in the garden.

"Time to go, lads." He brushed past them and started down the long path to the sea. His men scurried after him.

The walk from the temple to the port passed in stifled taciturnity and weariness, Rafe brooding in his thoughts until a tentative voice asked, "Are you all right, sir?"

Rafe looked at Short Davy in surprise. "What? Why do you ask?"

"Well, it's just you haven't done something like that in a long time. Not since…" He hesitated, but only briefly. "Not since Black Axe Morgan and his pirates. So, I was wondering if you're all right."

Rafe gave a small smile. "Yes, I'm fine. As well as any of us, I imagine. Thank you, Davy, for asking."

"That's good. Because I think we need you, sir, with your focus solely on what lies ahead. We're in for rough weather, I expect."

"Yes, we are." Rafe glanced at his two men, stalwart and true. His burden felt lighter. "And I'm glad to have you by my side and part of my crew. You two are good men."

A little pride swelled in Pinky and Short Davy, and they grinned. "We're honoured to serve, sir," Davy replied, and Pinky nodded his agreement. Then the trio fell into a comfortable silence, knowing they were united in purpose.

They emerged at the port to find a pacing Blackthorne with a look so grim and dark it made a soul wonder why he hadn't besieged the town with cannon fire. He shouted the moment he spied Rafe.

"Captain! At last! Thank the waves you're safe!"

Rafe grinned despite the circumstances. It was a rare thing to see Blackthorne agitated. "Yes, Blackthorne. I'm fine. How are things on the ship?"

"At the ready and awaiting your orders, sir!"

"Good." Rafe swung his attention to Short Davy and Pinky. "You two go aboard and take Angus if he's not already there. Blackthorne and I will be right behind—"

"Captain Morrow! A word before you depart." The voice of the harbourmaster interrupted, and he hurried over to Rafe in an agitated manner. "I couldn't let you leave without offering my heartfelt apologies. Such awful business. Terrible. I'm still in such a state over it. The whole port feels the loss. I, we, are in your debt, sir, and are profoundly sorry for the insult done to you." His face darkened, and his voice lowered. "And the sad tragedy of course. The Oracle was a kind and brave woman. She deserved better."

Rafe gave him a kind smile. "I appreciate the sympathies, sir. And the apology, though you and your people did nothing wrong. You can rest assured, you all still hold my favour."

"Thank you, Captain. Thank you."

Rafe glanced at his ship. "We should depart. We have much to do."

"Of course, I won't keep you further."

And with that, the harbourmaster took his leave while Rafe, Blackthorne, and the other men returned to the ship. A relieved but sombre crew greeted them.

Rafe gazed at their concerned faces. "I take it you've all heard?"

"Aye, Captain." One-Eyed Anders took a step forward. "'Tis a terrible loss. Will we be staying in port for a bit? To pay our respects?"

"I wish we could, but I'm afraid we have things that need tending to. Things that have been put off far too long. I've let events spiral off-kilter, but it's time to steer back to a truer course. We set sail, boys. We're heading out to the deep sea."

"What bearing should I lay in, Captain?"

"Our destination is the Isle of Shadows. The Gateway to the Gods." The words fell faster than a shot cannonball and hit the deck as hard.

Sharp gasps rose on a cloud of trepidation, and more than a few crew made warding signs against their chests. Rafe ignored the reaction. Instead, he summoned his magic, dark and yawning, and sunk its power deep into the frame, the hull, and the sail of the ship. The *Celestial Jewel* shook and squealed, a sound almost like a laugh.

Anders manned the wheel and navigated out of the harbour with quick ease. His hands shook on the wheel. The ship shuddered and picked up speed. Looks of consternation spread across the crew.

"Steady, lads. It will be a fast trip, but none to worry. She near to fly now, boys, and skim the waves like a knife through butter. It's on to the Isle of Shadows in but a few hours."

Anders didn't seem pleased or mollified. "Are you sure about this, Captain?"

"You have your orders, Mr. Anders. Take us out."

"Aye, sir," came his grumbling acceptance.

As the ship sailed from port, the angry cry of a crow echoed across the sky.

Chapter Seventeen
Isle of Shadows

With his ship sailing for open waters, Rafe stood at the prow, his feet firm on deck and the wind in his hair. Behind him, an unhappy crew worked but that didn't lessen his resolve. Events had led him straight to a reckoning with his family and he couldn't back down.

He heard footsteps behind him and smiled. He expected him sooner. "Speak your piece, Blackthorne."

Rafe heard a mumble of surprise and discomfiture and then the first mate's voice. "Are you certain of this course, sir? You know what happened last time you went there looking for help."

"I know, but I'm not seeking their help or approval this time. They can all be damned. This is just a formal declaration of war between me and my sister and whatever she allies herself with."

He sighed. "Besides, the last words of the Oracle

before she passed to the After World bade me to seek out my father." He turned to look at Blackthorne. "And the God of Souls cannot ignore her final words of counsel."

"When did she—" Blackthorne cut his question short, and an intake of breath floated past Rafe's ear. He wasn't certain whether it was surprise, fear, or admiration. Blackthorne then added, "They won't like your coming, sir."

"No, they won't. But they won't stop me, either. Not after what's happened and the ensuing consequences."

"Well, sir, sailing with you is never boring, I'll say that much."

Rafe chuckled. "Glad to do my part to keep your life lively, Blackthorne."

"I appreciate it, sir."

Rafe heard his footsteps fade away along the deck, and he was alone again. At least as alone as one could be standing on the deck of a busy ship of sailors. He heard grunts, a bit of swearing, the crank of pulleys as the sails were trimmed, voices calling out orders, and jokes and the thump and rumble of boots against the solid wood of the deck. He heard the sound of home far more so than their destination, the land where he spent most of his youth. He closed his eyes.

I pray their coming together doesn't blow them both apart.

He opened his eyes, his gaze once again back on the horizon and the sea.

The fog bank came into view first. Swirling tendrils and expanded puffs of pinkish vapour gliding against the sea like a lover's hand, caressing its surface. The diaphanous mist danced and swayed. Its contortions seeming playful, almost alive.

"We've arrived." The words rebounded to Rafe's crew, a statement soaked in whispering awe and echo. The captain walked the deck to the wheel, laying a hand on One-Eyed Anders' shoulder.

"Steady on the helm from here. Magic will be guiding you in. Let it flow. Don't fight it."

The man nodded. "Aye, Captain. I remember."

"Good man."

Rafe strode back to the prow, keeping an eye on the sea, watching the progress of the ship. He closed his eyes and gently siphoned off some of the magic from the *Jewel*. Finesse more than speed was needed now. The ship slowed her pace, steadying to a normal clip, and an overly taciturn crew manoeuvred through the fog. The air grew still, a silence fractured only by the vessel's creaks and groans and the slap of waves. As if the collective crew held its breath waiting for the end. As if the world itself slowed, the tick of time forgotten.

Too late to turn back now.

Once past the miasma barrier, the ship steered into cerulean waters and sunlight-tinged clouds. The wind smelled of sweet honey and the perfect warmth of the heart of summer sashayed over the crew. Calm sea, clear and sparkling, splashed against the sides of the vessel. And, above their heads, the bluest sky kissed dancing, vaporous shapes of feathery alabaster. They sailed into a paradise.

Yet the looming shape of the Isle of Shadows belied that notion. The great, disquieting beast of an island jutted on the horizon. A stain on the beauty. Dark and ominous, it warned away travellers, this Gateway to the Gods.

Even at first glance, it inspired dread. Its landmass shifted like an illusion in moonlight, an obsidian hue undulating through the sun. Edges shimmered and fluttered and slid against the sea like drifting tide. An outline the eye couldn't quite pin down. It could make a man believe in madness.

"What's going on? Did that island really move?" The fearful voice of Hugh broke the quiet.

"Yes." Rafe spoke softly to coax away the trepidation from the newest crew member. "The Isle of Shadows is constantly in motion as it vacillates between realms. Land, hills, harbours, and bays transform and disappear. It also makes heaving anchor at port difficult unless you're invited in."

"And we're going there?"

"Aye, lad. We are." Rafe stared at the isle with an unspoken sigh. Once his home, despite its vagaries and whims, he knew it well. He knew where to bring in his ship to hail his kin. He could feel the magic tremble under his feet, and he smiled. *The Jewel* would take them in. She knew.

"Five degrees to starboard, Mr. Anders, and hold her course steady."

Assured his orders would be followed, Rafe walked a few steps to the rail. He took a breath and held it between the worlds for a heartbeat of infinity. When the ship glided against the right spot in the sea, he exhaled a whisper of air, followed by the murmur of a name, "Cylla."

The prevailing winds quavered in response, a scintillation of sky and a taste of laughter, and the deck of the ship rumbled. From beneath the vast turquoise waters, an unbounded whirlpool surfaced in a spray of bubbled foam and spume. Beyond it all, from the ageless void and the timeless clouds, Cylla, Gatekeeper of the Isle of Shadows, cascaded downward on a floral scent and sunbeams. She halted inches above the whirlpool, a smile on her face

"Welcome home, God of Souls."

"Still with the grand entrance I see, Cylla."

A trill of laughter with the cadence of silver bells fluttered across the deck and into the sails. "Of course. I love a good spectacle." Her smile widened. "What do you want from me this day? An audience with one of your brethren?"

He hesitated, for a brief moment, not knowing how his next words would be received. "I want entrance to the isle, Cylla. I have a declaration of war against the Moon Goddess."

An audible crack reverberated as if the air itself split. Waves slapped the sides of the ship and spray erupted from the whirlpool. But Cylla said nothing.

Rafe answered her nonetheless. "Flexing your power won't change what I need to do, aunt. My sister has gone too far this time in her madness. There are forces at play that cannot be ignored. You had to have felt the repercussions, even here."

"I did. And the others have been... unnerved by the ripples, this change in the balance of magic."

"And yet no one cared to ask what happened or why." Rafe snorted. "Better to stay here, tucked away from any consequences. Well, this time they cannot hide. The consequences have come to them."

Cylla hung her head, concealing her expression, but he heard her whisper. "But war, God of Souls? Has it come to this?"

"Yes, Cylla. It has come to war. The first salvo has already happened. The first battles have already been fought." He let out a sighing breath. "It cannot be halted anymore one way or the other. Will you let me and mine through? Do we have entry to the Isle of Shadows?"

This time she looked at him, her eyes shining with tears, and sorrow etched on her face. "Yes, you have entry. Sail the whirlpool through to the isle." And she ascended back to the sky and clouds.

"You heard her, Mr. Anders! Sail straight ahead into the heart of the whirlpool!"

"Aye, Captain!" came the answer, and the *Jewel* cut a path into the churning, spinning waters. The ship bucked like a frenzied beast and the shower of seafoam touched as high as the sails.

From behind, the captain issued Hugh's scream of, "Are you mad?" and Rafe chuckled. "Not yet, Mr. Corbin, not yet!"

The entire crew braced as they entered the maelstrom, but if Hugh or anyone imagined being tossed and torn by the fierce eddy of the whirlpool, or smashed beneath the surface, their expectations ended in relieved disappointment. The ship sailed smoothly as if in calm seas, straight and true, settling into the centre of the vortex.

Then the ship began to sink.

One foot. Two feet. Three. Down, down as the sides of the cyclone of sea rose around them like a cocoon so close, a person could reach out and touch the swirling water, although no sane being would try.

Rafe stood at the prow, anticipation running fire through his blood. "Hold on boys, we're about to move!"

A caroming lurch shuddered from the bowels of the ship and beyond, shaking bones of ship and crew and rattling teeth and tack. The vessel powered forward, cradled in the sea of a prison that carried it as if under its own sail. The roiling undertow of water glided through the choppy tide with ease, and the *Celestial Jewel* came to harbour in a sheltered bay of the island. The whirlpool dissolved, settling the ship to tranquil waters and rocking it gently in the secluded haven.

Behind him, Rafe could feel the fretful angst of the crew, given voice without warning by Hugh Corbin. "Did we...? Did that happen? How is that even possible?" His words caressed the heavens with a plaintive appeal.

Rafe chuckled, despite it all. "We did, Mr. Corbin. We did. We sailed the whirlpool gate to the Isle of Shadows. Courtesy of the capricious nature and magic of the gods." He turned his head to look at the dead sailor. A flabbergasted man stared back as if the ghost had seen a ghost. "You'd best get used to strange occurrences, Mr. Corbin, sailing on this ship."

"I believe I'm beginning to understand that, sir. And what peculiarities come next?"

"Nothing so strange, but waiting. From here I go ashore alone." He tilted his head to the stern. "Weigh anchor, gents, and lower the longboat."

The clattering clank of the anchor chains and the creak of the boat pulleys gave answer, and soon the captain rowed in solitary rhythm to the beach. He pulled the boat far above the high-water mark to avoid any playful and whimsical tide. As he stepped away, a shilly-shally of wind twirled the sand at his feet. A giggle sounded close to his ear. Rafe smiled, despite everything.

"Is that you, Aryna?"

Another giggle and then, "Of course, brother."

"Come to play at the seashore, Wind Goddess? Swirl the salt air and toss the waves?"

"Where else would I be on such a beautiful day? To soar the sky and spin the sea foam." The sand spun a whirlwind, and in bright laughter, Aryna, Goddess of the Wind, made herself visible. Her light silver hair was longer than he remembered, but her taste in diaphanous gowns had not changed.

"As lovely as ever, sister." He gave a slight bow and she giggled. "Do you know why I've come? Did they send you?"

"No to both questions, brother. I go where I wish. No one sends me. You know this."

"I do. But please tell me, where are the others, Aryna? Together or scattered about the island?" A regretful and resentful sigh crept into his tone, and emotional shadows crossed his face.

Aryna gave a pout. "Oh dear, so grim. Have you come to spoil my day, brother?"

"I'm afraid so. Where are they, sister?"

"They're all gathered at the old stone temple. I suppose you're the reason. They've been there for days, milling about like lost sheep, muttering about disturbances in the balance. I finally fled their gloom. What does it matter? Catastrophes, shifts in power, the world always rights itself in the end." She laughed and the wind fluttered her hair.

"Not this time. The Moon Goddess has gone too far this time. She means to destroy everything. And she's gained the power to accomplish her goal."

"Don't be silly. She wouldn't destroy everything. That would be—"

"Madness." Rafe finished her sentence. Aryna had the grace to look discomfited. "She sent the Kraken to attack the Sea Portal, sister. To enter the After World. And she attacked me directly."

A sharp intake of breath akin to a gale through a sea cave answered his words. Aryna wilted, her form fading to translucent. "She wouldn't. She couldn't."

"She did."

"No. No. I don't want to listen." She ebbed even further, disappearing from sight in a flurry of summer breeze. "They're at the temple. Tell them. Let them handle her."

Rafe sighed. Aryna always lived up to his low expectations. Her variable nature constantly kept her flying and unwilling to face problems.

No point in dwelling, though. I still have to confront the rest.

He walked on, across the beach towards the lush forest. The trees shimmered, almost beckoning him, their form wavering halfway between tropical splendour and evergreens. As he drew nearer, the underbrush parted, and the ancient path appeared.

"Showing me the way, how kind." Rafe smiled and nodded to the verdant forest.

Trees pulled back their branches, vines separated, and the trail became unimpeded. Rafe ambled off the beach, traipsing through the island foliage.

The light filtered through the flora, cavorting with shadows on the leaves and flowers. The sweet smell of honey dripped, melding into the sylvan scent of the eternal blooms. A sultry heat glided along the wind currents, and Rafe removed his coat. He walked in idyllic grandeur, accompanied by the dulcet songs of the birds and an occasional rustle in the brush until he arrived at the stone temple.

There, the beauty of the elemental woodlands met a small clearing, surrounded by a grove of fragrant smelling fruit trees and blooming bushes of crimson flowers. In its centre, stood a building made of grey stone elevated on a black stone foundation. It boasted a colonnade front and an arched roof with a trail of ivy snaking about its girth. Not a grandiose structure. No adornment or etched designs. Simply a rectangular building tucked beneath the clear blue skies and secluded among the trees. Yet, the air around it tingled, almost glittered. He hesitated at the edge of the glade, staring at the temple.

So many memories of this place. So few of them good. Now I add to the pain. I wonder what awaits me inside?

With a sigh, Rafe walked forward and climbed the set of stone steps to the entrance. He laid his hand on the door, leaving it there for a brief moment, and then pushed it open. The silence of everlasting darkness greeted him. The thick gloom between the realm of the gods and the world of men. It extended down a winding corridor lined with white marble columns and indecipherable whispers. He went in and closed the door behind him.

"So, I am here."

His voice didn't echo. The inky black swallowed it. Adding it to its collection of reverberating undertones.

Rafe moved onward, treading through the darkness, chased by murmurs past the edge of sight. The ebony shadows enclosed him in a cocoon, extending a path cushioned in obscurity and blindness, but he knew the way and needed no sight to guide him. On muted footsteps, he made his way to the inner sanctum and stepped over the pitch black threshold of the world beyond. The world he was born into. The world he left behind.

An illuminated doorway imbued with blue-streaked light marked the end of the passage: the entrance to the chamber of the gods. Arched and opaque, it glowed a soft and radiant amber, suspended between the particles of connecting black. Light spilled into the sooty ether and cycled from a subsisting arcane core. The door stood as a palpitating sentry, a route from one realm to another imbued with magic and power. And like all good doors, locked against intruders.

Rafe laid his hand on the undulating surface, the luminosity cold to his skin. For a moment, the chill lingered then pulsed and changed to warmth under his fingers. The light danced along the edge of itself, sending sparks into the darkness, and an oscillating hum broke the silence. The magic wriggled up his arm and sang to the power in his own blood. With a gentle trill, the illumination shimmered to transparent and vanished, leaving an opening to the realm beyond. With a sigh, Rafe walked through the gateway.

Soft violet mist greeted him, tingling where it touched his skin, swirling around his body as he moved farther into the realm of the gods. He finally stepped from betwixt the worlds into the temple's private gathering hall, a stark, rotund room of white.

His family awaited him.

The first to turn at his arrival, facing him with a scowl, was his father. The great Reis, Sovereign of the Gods. He advanced to confront Rafe. "What in all the realms were you thinking, closing the Portal of the Sea!"

"Delightful to see you, Father, as always." Rafe left the bitter in his words. Too much had passed between them to spare feelings anymore.

Before Reis answered, a flurry of movement pushed forward and his sister, Bevire, Goddess of Shadows and Night, appeared. She sneered at Rafe. "Still disrespectful, I see, and arrogant. You don't even have the decency to come as one of us but in this guise of a mortal. How dare you show your face after abandoning everything, your family, your name, your home!"

Long festering anger seethed inside Rafe. "Abandoning you? That's not how I remember it. I was exiled, sister! Stop rewriting the past."

"Be quiet!" His father's commanding voice interrupted the conversation, and the bickering pair fell silent. Reis repeated his query. "Why did you seal the gateway to the After World?"

"Yes! Answer the question!" Bevire snapped off one more gibe at her brother.

Rafe glared, a hurricane of resentment plastered on his face. "You already know why! You just refuse to accept the truth!" Rafe let all his anger and his power show. His family took a step back as the temple sparked in raw blue energy. "Manume! The mad Goddess of the Moon! My sister! Your daughter! She sent her Kraken spawn to the portal! To destroy the After World and consume every soul there! I did what was necessary to protect my domain!" Rafe took a breath and glared, daring anyone to naysay him. "I did my duty as a god, which is more than I can say for any of you."

Reis' scowl deepened, and whispers slid among the other deities. Bevire sniffed, "I don't believe it. You must have overreacted. This mess is simply between you and our sister. It doesn't involve us."

"Not anymore." Rafe met her disdain with his own. "Something has shifted in the balance of power. You may think it is safe, hiding here while Manume wreaks havoc in the mortal world, but you can't hide anymore. Something else has stirred from the darkness."

Bevire shot him an incredulous look, but Rafe noticed his father's worried brow. His tone softened as he added, "Both our worlds are in danger. Whatever the reason, her creatures have attacked shrines and towns. They've broken their bindings. If you think you are immune to her madness, you are wrong. She's coming for us all. I believe whatever aids her means to destroy all realms."

"You are spouting ridiculous prattle," Bevire snorted. "And what do I care of shrines and towns? Your talk is nothing but fanciful nonsense conjured from folly! Do you have proof she works with outside forces? Do you? That this is more than just your continual feud?"

"Only the fact Manume attacked me directly and came within a wind's whisper of beating me." He let the shock of that statement sink in and then added, "If Lynna hadn't intervened, I would have lost the battle." He glared at Bevire. "Now tell me she does not have aid in her latest madness."

Bevire gasped. "You lie! That can't be true! I won't believe it!"

"Believe what you like. It makes no difference. I did not come here to debate. I am simply declaring my intent of war." He let the words wash over the assembled company of gods, and saw another shocked hush settle on those gathered. "I would ask your help, but I will fight her regardless of whether you grant it."

His father was the first to speak. "It has truly come to this?"

"Yes."

Rafe watched Reis close his eyes and let out a breath that contained an infinite scope of sorrow, regret, and pity. "Such was my fear. I wished it not to be so, but my bones told me otherwise." Another soft, lingering sigh. "So be it. Do you plan to end her existence? Safeguards will have to be put in place for subsequent ramifications if you plan on taking her life."

"I considered it, but as you said, ramifications..." Rafe grimaced in distaste, a harsh and sour gesture. "A death battle between us could do everlasting harm to the realms."

"Then what is this nonsense about war!" Bevire slung another barb but with far less confidence this time.

"There is no nonsense, this war has been coming for a very long time. I may not mean to kill her, but I will defeat her, and whatever else stands in my way. The destructive reign of the Goddess of the Moon ends! Her power as a goddess will end!" He put bravado into the words, even knowing they were hollow. He had no idea how to stop his sister.

Exclamations resounded off the walls from all the assembled gods, guttural noises of shock and spat words laced with indignation and disgust. Rafe ignored it all. He was watching his father's reaction.

His father stared, melancholy and relief etched in his expression, his mouth pursed in not quite a frown. Then a look akin to resignation flickered in his eyes. "If you mean to do that, you'll need the Ankara Stone."

More gasps charged the room, and Bevire shrieked, "You can't give him that!"

Reis turned to his daughter. "I can do what I like." The soft tone belied the warning in his voice, but Bevire ceased her protest.

Satisfied, Reis closed his hand and it glowed with an exquisite silver light. A luminescence so beautiful it rivalled the spark of twinkling starlight scattered across a halcyon sea. The warmth and scent of a blossom coated summer wind infused the hall, and the notes of a honeyed song older than the islands serenaded their ears.

After a few minutes, Reis opened his hand and the magic ceased. On his palm, sat a circular stone, pearl-white and two inches in diameter. "Take it. Use it wisely and as you will."

Rafe stared at the stone, at his father. A realization snapped to his mind. "You knew. You knew all along." Accusations dripped off his tongue with his words.

"The world cannot shift this much without my knowledge, God of Souls. Of course, I knew. But knowing and believing are far apart sometimes." Reis stepped closer, leaned in and whispered in his son's ear. "And some knowledge cannot be acted on. The worlds are far more complex than you wish to believe. Destinies are built on choices, and this destiny was never mine." Reis stepped back and held his hand.

Confused and angry, nevertheless, Rafe plucked the stone from his father's outstretched palm. It felt cold and light. He held it between his fingertips and studied its glittering surface.

I could destroy them all with this.

The quiet of the damned blanketed the room save for the anxious whimper of Bevire. They all waited on him. Rafe inhaled, let the breath out, and placed the stone in his pocket.

"Thank you, Father."

"You were right. From the beginning." The words surprised Rafe, and the sad smile on his father's face acknowledged the admittance laden within the words. "This has to be done. It should have been done a long time ago. I wish you fair winds and a stronger spirit than mine in this task, my son."

Rafe bowed his head, in respect of his father and of his tacit confession of guilt. When he raised his head, their eyes met in a locked gaze of sadness as deep and wide as any ocean. Rafe circled about and left the temple without another word.

The beach was empty as he returned to the longboat. No sister or summer winds ruffled the sands of the shoreline. He rowed back to the *Jewel* on placid seas and clambered aboard amid barely audible sighs of relief.

"Is it time to weigh anchor and be rid of this place, sir?"

"Aye, Blackthorne. I got what I came for. Turn her about and head west. The seas will lay in our course and head us home."

Chapter Eighteen
The Sea of Perpetual Moon

"Well, it's done. And for once they agreed without much fuss." Rafe poured himself a second glass of brandy. Blackthorne, sitting on the other side of his desk in the captain's quarters, still sipped on a first glass. Around them, the gentle rhythm of the sea rocked the boat like a tranquillity before the coming squall.

"So, it's a go then, sir? We're truly moving against the Moon Goddess?"

"Yes. May all the stars and seas help us, but yes."

"What's it to be then? A direct assault? Begging your pardon, sir. I know she's your sister, but will we be using lethal force and putting an end to her? It didn't fare well the last time we battled her."

"Now that would make it simple, wouldn't it? One battle, winner takes all. But as in most things, Blackthorne, this endeavour won't be that simple. We kill her, and shockwaves will shiver throughout the realms with serious consequences for magic. Possibly catastrophic, permanent consequences. In addition, her death leaves her monstrous children unchecked. She dies, and whatever's left of the spells that bind their actions, could snap. Her death could very likely leave them roaming free creating mindless havoc."

"Not a happy thought. So how do we fight her?"

"That, my friend, is where the affair gets tricky." Rafe swirled his brandy and took a sip. "We're not going to fight her. We're going to abduct her."

Blackthorne barely managed to keep from choking on his brandy. "We're going to what?!" In his agitation, he didn't even notice the drop of liquor and spittle running down his chin. "That's lunacy, even for you!"

Rafe chuckled at his first mate's flustered insubordination. "Isn't it just? But we're going to do it nonetheless. Don't worry I have a plan."

Blackthorne muttered, "That's when I worry most," and downed his remaining brandy in one gulp.

Rafe chuckled again. "Oh, I think you'll like it, Blackthorne." He slipped the Ankara stone out of his pocket and held it to the gaze of his first mate.

"What is that?" Blackthorne's knuckles whitened as he gripped his empty glass.

"The key to everything, my friend." With a smile, Rafe leaned in and laid out his scheme in detail. By the end of the recitation, Blackthorne's face reflected admiration, disbelief, and a hint of terror.

"I was right. It is lunacy. But a lunacy that may work, sir. With skill and a great deal of luck."

Rafe smiled. "Well then, here's to luck and skill." He raised his glass and finished his brandy.

The *Jewel* came into port late the next day at Tenby Key to weather the night and restock supplies from the disgruntled and fearful townsfolk. Word of the Oracle's death and what happened after had spread. Not a person looked at Rafe without discomfort.

The dark night seemed to swallow that unease as the captain stood on deck, his thoughts swirling, Blackthorne by his side.

"Not an attack by any monster since you battled your sister, sir. They say the seas are quiet."

"That's a blessing at least. And tomorrow we sail to see that they stay that way."

"Aye, sir. May all the luck of the islands be with us."

Rafe chuckled an unhappy sound. "We'll need it." He glanced at his first mate. "Go below and get some rest. We'll need that too."

Blackthorne hesitated. "What about you, sir?"

"I'll retire soon. Don't fuss."

"Yes, sir." And Rafe listened to the man's retreating footsteps and stared at the stars.

In the early dawn of the morning, the ship left port and navigated for open waters, headed to places even the gods feared. Hour after hour, they sailed far past the boundaries defining the Outer Island territories, past where the edges of the After World met the vast ocean, and beyond the threshold of the gods' domain. The ship navigated from the familiar lilt and rock of the known seas to the wild expanse of the briny deep where madness and aberration made its home. The waters where the magic of the moon and sea monsters held dominion.

In his usual spot, Rafe stood at the prow looking to the horizon. Behind him, he heard snatches of conversation between One-Eyed Anders at the helm and the newest crew member, Hugh Corbin.

"Are we truly going to confront the Moon Goddess? After what happened?"

"Aye, we are. Sailing straight to the Mists of Infinity we are, a swirling mass of fog that'll steal your wits and have a ship sailing aimlessly in its tendrils 'til the end of time itself. And we got to cross it to get to where she lives, the Sea of Perpetual Moon."

"Perpetual moon?"

"Aye. Been there only once myself. A long time ago, and in a different life. Nothing but dusk and gloom and the shining moon. The Goddess lives on one of the isles in the Archipelago of Nightfall. Surely you heard about that place. All the stories about them islands make up half the legends spouted by the old salts."

"That I know. The archipelago is infamous. The Isle of Bones, Ruins Key, the Island of Stone, the Ghastly Reef, the Sanctuary of Shadows, Obscurity Atoll, and the Haven of Despair."

"Aye. All those and many that have never made it into the stories. Captain says it's the place where the gods were born and where things older than this world once lived. Having seen it, I believe him. It ain't a natural place, not a place for mortals like us."

"But still we sail there."

"Ain't got no choice, have we? Don't know how else to stop her."

The conversation fell silent, and Rafe inwardly sighed. He wished they could turn back, but nothing could prevent what would happen. They sailed on as if on a pleasure cruise until the first tendrils of mist wisped across the sea.

Rafe gave a shout. "Mists of Infinity, dead ahead. Sound the bell and keep it ringing!"

Quiet Peter clanged the ship's bell at a steady interval as the ship entered the mystical fog bank. The air trembled with each peal, pushing outward into the fog, shoving it back and clearing a path through the miasma. Moaning rebounded off the breeze and the haze, and the faint swish of other ships on the water, though no shapes or souls could be seen.

"What's out there?" The tiny, frightened cry from Mouse voiced every fear.

"The long lost past, son, and nothing we can do about it." Rafe's voice held pity and grief. "Try not to listen. We won't be joining them as long as the bell tolls."

And true sailing, they did. With each clang of the bell, the mist parted, and they came out the other side into the Sea of Perpetual Moon. The soft, inky watercolour of dusk surrounded them with the twinkling of stars and the light of the moon overhead.

Gasps drifted on the final notes of the ship's bell, and Rafe spoke a few words of reassurance. "'Tis only magic, men. A realm where the moon never strays from the sky. We've sailed worse." An uneasy calm settled on the crew, and they struck a new heading, straight towards the Archipelago of Nightfall, the lair of the Moon Goddess.

The *Jewel* cut smoothly through the waters, and the sea stretched on as clear and as dark as black glass. From an eternal twilight sky, the lunar light skidded off the surface of the water, mirroring the stars. The pale orb peeked from behind the scanty clouds. Radiance shone like gossamer hairs settling in the wind. Rafe stared at the sky, studying the pale light, admiration and dread warring in his soul.

"Such a thing of beauty, sister, that you have in your care. And yet, you've made it ugly." He let his whisper fly on a hint of hope and regret. The moon shimmered without answer, silver blue nestled in indigo velvet, a nimbus of frost and gleam, of tinted pearl and silvery sparkle. As if his own echo, Rafe murmured, "Such a beauteous thing, through time and tide," and turned his gaze back to the sea.

Mr. Blackthorne approached him on deck, a grim face and no glances for the moon. "All is prepared, Captain. As well as we're able. We'll give a good fight when it comes to it."

"Pray it doesn't come to it, Mr. Blackthorne, though I fear it will. Pray we manage to catch her unawares and without her monstrous followers." The fingers of Rafe's right hand curled into a fist. "Or whatever else aids her."

"I have been, sir, and will continue to pray. To every and any god that will hear me. But you may be the only one listening."

Rafe spun a rueful smile. "I may be, Mr. Blackthorne. Let us hope I am up to the task then, shall we?"

"If I were a betting man, sir, I'd wager on you every time. Even in this lunacy." And with those words, Mr. Blackthorne gave the captain a nod and took his leave with a smile.

Rafe watched him go. A mix of pride, affection, and trepidation followed the first mate's footsteps and he turned and scanned the horizon. Soon, they'd be arriving at their rendezvous with his sister.

Soon, their plan to abduct the Moon Goddess would commence.

Chapter Nineteen
The Moon and Monsters

The smell of the air rippled in metallic quintessence, overlaid with salt, seaweed, blight, and rot. The seawater burbled and swelled grey and green, slapping angrily against the sides of the vessel. Slimy tendrils of a new sickly fog snaked across the ocean, its fingers reaching out to entwine and grasp at the bowels of the ship.

Rafe glanced over the rail and watched the mist encircle them. "Blighted fog's coming in, boys." His voice cast soft, but far to every ear. "It'll get worse from here on out. Cut the sail and come in slow and careful."

Like silent cats, the crew obeyed, and the *Jewel* dropped speed. They kept the course, drifting gently through the waves and fog, the air ever thickening in their forward momentum until velvet banks of haze swallowed the space around them. It blotted the sky and moon, cutting visibility to only a few feet.

"Steady now, Mr. Anders!" In a sotto voice, Rafe barked the command to the man at the helm, and then, to his crew, gave the order, "Trim the sail and slow her down more! We want her creeping along in this fog. It wouldn't do to stumble upon a sea beastie without warning."

In quick order, the crew complied and the ship slowed to a crawl through the water. The grey vapour puffed like fat floating pillows, spinning past sailor and ship, cold and clammy as it brushed by. Silver strands of moonlight trickled through the cover, casting diffused and grotesque shadows in the undying night.

The shaky voice of Mouse whispered, "Do you think there are ghosts out there?"

"We are the ghosts, sonny," came the answering jest of Pinky Jasper with an accompanying chuckle.

Then, from a spot beyond the wall of fog, drifted the cackle of a female voice and a string of peculiar nattering tantamount to incoherent rambling. And far in the distance, growing ever fainter, the cawing of a crow.

Against the ear of One-Eyed Anders, Rafe whispered, "Bring her three degrees to port."

Gripping the wheel as if it was his salvation against doom and perdition, Anders complied. The ship angled silently into the new heading.

The *Jewel* pushed through the fog, fighting the current, lurching against the swell, as the sea seemed to thicken and curdle into black soup. Icy fingers of wind and murk clutched at the crew and the ship as they stole forward inch by inch against dusky, slurping waters that matched the raven sky peering between the hoary gloom. And echoing from the distance, came undulating cries.

"Monsters." The quavering whisper of Mouse broke the unnatural quiet.

"Aye," Rafe answered, his voice barely audible, "but not close. Keep on the heading, Mr. Anders. Not much farther, I think."

The ship sailed on, her pale outline swallowed in the fog, making her more of a phantom ship than ever before. She prowled the black seas, a silent predator hunting and being hunted. The crew kept her steady, their collective mind on task, focused and vigilant. Muscles strained, clenched jaws strangled any banter, and whitening knuckles played the ropes as friction coagulated the air and atmosphere.

Then a flicker of moonlight beckoned out of the fog, the pea-soup thinning allowing eyes to see the shine on the horizon line. Anticipation slid in on that light.

"Look lively, boys. We're coming out of it, into the fire. Prepare the harpoons and the nets. Mouse," the boy set to quivering at the sound of his name. "Run below deck and tell the gunners to make ready the cannon." The lad scurried away, set on his duty, and the rest of the crew primed for war.

The *Jewel* glided out of the fog soon after, into a calm

expanse of sea. The wind abruptly died away, strangled into stillness, and all noise dissolved into the hush. Nary a usual sound could be heard, not waves on wood nor the soft flap of the sail. Even the breath of the crew faded into the dead air. Only the forward momentum of the ship kept the *Jewel* moving.

"Doldrums." A nameless voice dropped the word like a stone, the fear rippling across the deck. Whispers drifted from man to man.

"No wind."

"What'll we do?"

"We'll be stranded."

"Easy prey."

"By all the seas..."

The bones of the ship creaked as her speed slowed in the stillness until she was barely moving at all. Rafe looked at his crew. Fear had chased away all else. Rafe wanted to speak, but the oppressive quiet seemed to have stolen his voice.

Almost suspended, both in ship and men, the *Jewel* awaited something, anything. A whine, barely audible, and a splash broke the spell.

A chill shivered its way through Rafe's blood, and he dashed to the rail and scanned the waters, reaching out with every sense he had, magical or otherwise. Sure enough, a frisson of power shifted in the air.

"Man the weapons!" No sooner than the words left

his mouth did the seas undulate and ripple, the clear signs of movement barrelling toward the ship illuminated by the moonlight. "Man those weapons! We have sea monsters heading in!"

His cries fractured the tense calm into chaos, organized and efficient, but screaming chaos. Waves swamped the ship, sweeping across deck, and shadows rose from the water into form. In spray and salt, beasts leapt from the ocean, arcing through the air to slam on deck with a thud, and a screech of rage.

Rafe drew his sword and shouted, "We've been boarded! All hands on deck!"

Chapter Twenty
Attack!

Rafe rushed forward, hacking at the tentacles of the nearest sea monster, which slithered out of reach before the blade connected. Another shout echoed behind him as he regrouped, and other men stepped into the fray.

"Bloody hell! It's a pack of scuttle-squid!"

And indeed, seven fearsome creatures squirmed and darted over the wet deck boards, their crab-like pincers snapping, their tentacles grasping, and their quick clacking movements evading blade and club. They swarmed the sailors not manning harpoons or cannons.

Rafe rushed the beasts and attacked the nearest who hissed and gnashed its toothy jaws at One-Eyed Anders. Rafe slashed its eye with his sword and yelled, "Give them no quarter, men! Send them back to the depths!"

An answering bellow came from the wounded creature and it reared up, lashing out with its razor-sharp pincers. Rafe dodged, his foot slipping on the wet deck. The broad side of a claw slammed into his chest, knocking him off his feet.

Rafe's shoulder and side crashed into the wooden deck, and he sucked in a painful breath. Hearing the rush of clattering appendages, he rolled, ending face up. The spectacle of a leaping scuttle-squid filled his vision and *Thwack!* A sword swished over his head and cut into the beast, shell and sliced tentacles flying. One severed tentacle smacked into a mast, before sliding across the deck. Mouse charged the now floundering monster again, bringing his bloodied sword down repeatedly and hacking the creature into pieces. Blood, meaty flesh, and gore spread a slick film over the deck interspersed with scattered bits of rank squid intestine. Rafe gaped at the sight and gagged from the smell.

Then One-Eyed Anders bellowed, "Bloody hell! The world is ending! Mouse just killed a scuttle-squid!"

The boy giggled wildly, and the captain recovered his wits. He roared, "Look lively you two! We've still a battle to win. Back to duty!"

The two scurried off, and Rafe scrambled to his feet, taking care not to slip on squid innards. He retrieved his sword and jumped back into the fray. The deck was awash in gore, the air clinging with a putrid mix of bile, spoiled fish, blood, and salt sea. Shrieks, roars, grunts, and curses clashed with the swish of blades, the thunk of clubs, and the thwack of steel slicing into flesh.

"Give them no quarter, boys!" Rafe's sword sliced through the air, arching down into the head of an advancing scuttle-squid, flinging brain matter as he whirled and cut into a wolf eel chomping on the rail. Entrails splashed the deck as the fish creature was carved open stem to stern. Then a black sea wyrm burst from the water, wings flapping, only to be met with the sharp edge of Rafe's weapon. Blood showered the ship, and bits of raw flesh clung to Rafe's coat and hair.

The captain glanced around, seeing more bloodied steel and inhaling the smell of gunpowder. Dead beasts littered his ship, but the crew was holding its own. Rafe smiled. "We'll win this fight! Do you hear me, sister, we'll win!"

A roar came from the sea, answered by the crack of cannon fire from the *Jewel*. Another bellow and the sea turned red. A myriad of screams echoed off the water.

"Death to the beasts!" Anders' shout shook the sails, and the crew cheered.

Rafe raised his sword high in reply to his crewman's shout. "Aye, death to the beasts!" and then set to backing the words with actions. Side by side, Rafe and his crew stirred mayhem across deck and in the seas, dealing death to their monstrous attackers in a fury of gunfire cannon shot and cold steel. Until naught but creature corpses stained the ship, and the remaining monsters fled.

"We've got the beasties on the run!"

More cheers rose to the sky, and indeed, the creatures retreated.

For the moment.

Still, Rafe let out a sigh of relief and looked around, his breath coming quick and his heart pounding. He saw scattered mess and chaos and injured men, but none dead or eaten as far as he could tell. And yes, for a moment they had a respite.

He knew it wouldn't last. He could feel her presence lurking past the edges of the sea and moonlight. Rafe wiped his blood-smeared blade on his sleeve and sheathed the sword. From his pocket, he pulled the Ankara Stone and dropped it in his left hand. It pulsed, and a warm tingle surged across his skin, its weight and power pressing into his palm.

He took a breath. *It's all or nothing.*

He summoned the magic in his blood, the power flowing upward into his skin and mingling with the stone. Blue arcs of light sparked off the gem's surface, and it glowed in a sapphire radiance matching his own. His palm burned, and he clamped his jaw against the pain, hissing the binding words through his teeth.

"Dywch ar werc! Ymerch endr urd!"

A flash of luminescence and the gem transmuted into energy. It hovered for a moment, a ball of light cradled in his hand, and then melted into his flesh. Power coursed through bone and blood, and he gasped with the surge of sheer force now at his command.

He looked out across the sea and smiled. With a toss of his head and a reckless dash across the deck, Rafe grabbed a line and swung himself onto the rail, balancing precariously.

"It's time for a reckoning, sister!" His shout careened past the moonlight, off the swells and shrieking monsters, straight to the ears of the Moon Goddess.

She answered with cackling laughter.

Suddenly, the sea was awash with a brilliant silver moonbeam, and she appeared in the sky, to the port side of the ship. She hovered, illuminated in pale, white radiance and robes the colour of a summer sky, her silver hair wildly flowing. All eyes fixed on her, Manume: the fearsome Goddess of the Moon.

"Little brother, little brother! Come to play? Here I am waiting! Will we battle? Yes, we will! Battle! Battle! Make the stars quake and the seas rattle!"

She flew past the ship on moonlight and whirlwind to open sea. Her beasts silenced their screeching and sank beneath the surface of the ocean. She floated there in the distance, three feet above the sea, arms spread, a crooked smile on her face.

"Come and play, oh, brother!"

Rafe whispered, "I'm coming," and leapt from the rail of his ship.

Chapter Twenty One
A Reckoning

The sea air greeted him like wings above the dark waters. On a cascade of blue light and magic energy, he descended to the sea, halting inches above its surface. He hovered for a moment, and then Rafe propelled himself across the ocean's surface towards his sister. He skimmed the surface, sending a spray of water in his wake, and came to a stop five feet from his sister. He drifted upward until they were both the same height over the water.

"Your madness ends here, sister. No more mortals die. No more souls will be devoured. We end this."

"So brave. So brave. But no match, no match. Did you forget?"

Rafe smiled. "No. But you may be surprised this time."

"Tricks or clever words? No matter." She spun around with a laugh. "It's you or me, little brother. You and me. Always been. Always been. Yes, yes. One or the other. You or me." In an instant, her glee turned to a roar, a strident shriek of hopeless perception and pain-fuelled rage. White hot incandescence filled the sky and the space between them, churning the sea below their feet.

"You or me! At the end!" The furious energy burst forward, hurtling towards Rafe like a hurricane.

He barely shielded in time, but the force of her magic still flung him through the sky like a child's toy. In panting breath and flailing limbs, he righted himself and whirled back to face her. She snarled, the growl echoing across the divide that separated them, another bolt of energy slashing at Rafe.

He dodged her blow and threw a taunt back on the wind. "Is that all you have, sister? Weak. Very weak. My turn."

Electric fire pulsed from his fingertips and streaked across the sky in a lightning fast arc to strike at his sister. She spun away, but the energy's edge caught her arm, tumbling her into the ocean, all white light and spuming water. In an ejecting fountain of sea and shrieks, she re-emerged, chasing the clouds upwards. Her shrieks reverberated wide and far along the archipelago.

"No, no, no, no! Not strong! Not anymore!" She lifted her head and wailed, her words shattering the clouds above her and then swivelled to stare down her brother. "I hate you! Why can't I ever be rid of you?"

"You will never be rid of me, sister!" Rafe raced forward on blue glimmers and vapour to intercept her, tapping into the Ankara stone as he soared.

The sky around him glowed in a deep cerulean luminescence, and the air shimmered in primal magic. Dragged in his wake and from beneath the sea, rose a song born of loss. A final lament. The last dirge of the departed.

The voices of lost sailors, of lives murdered, snuffed from existence, of souls forever obliterated wailed. The unfathomable sorrow of buried misery ascended from the watery depths, the indelible echo of sentience erased. Long dead tongues shrieked notes of bereavement, of something precious, stolen from the world. The sound burst from the sea in a fury, a maelstrom fuelled by Rafe's magic, and shot like an arrow at the Goddess of the Moon, guided by Rafe's desire. He slung the overwhelming force at his sister.

With a snarl, she tried to counter with a magic energy of her own, but the song smashed through her shielding. White sparks and yowls struck her a palatable blow and her body shuddered before spinning like a whirlpool. She screamed and flew erratically across the sky, plummeting towards the water below. She skidded across the surface alight in sound and friction, Rafe's magic shivering along her skin.

"Make it stop! Make it stop!"

"I cannot." Rafe closed his eyes and whispered, *"Inacean arian, inacean arantu, inacean arandraich arfadh tamil."*

Filaments of white emerged from his hands, weaving themselves into a wider strip of energy. One more whispered word, *"Taighe"* and the power darted into the air, seeking his sister.

Tortured by the resurrected voices and their weeping requiem, she had no defence for Rafe's new attack. The strand of magic flitted through the air and wrapped around her throat, tightening into a circle on her skin. It penetrated into her blood and bone, spearing through the fibre of her magic. It throttled and blocked the conduits of her power, breaking the bonds between her mind and her innate, god-fuelled energy.

Her final scream reverberated off the fabric of the world and beyond, with an answering echo bellowed from the After World. All the voices of drowned shipwrecked sailors and their kin. Her own name shrieked in her ears, the anger and fear of the dead and the vanished singing in her head. Vile words beat at her, accusations, slurs, and pleas pierced her like barbs, sapping her magic, bleeding her dry. Piece by piece, she surrendered. Piece by piece the Ankara Stone's magic repressed her power. She dropped from the sky like a tossed rock.

Yet, as she fell, deep within her thoughts, Manume heard the echoing caw of a crow, and a sliver of red slipped beyond the sight of gods. Then the sea engulfed her.

The shock of the cold water brought her to her

senses, and the voices disappeared. She swam upward, breaking the surface to see her brother hovering above her.

She yelped a squeal of rage that quivered the substance of the world from the depths of the ocean to the clouds above. "No, no, no! How did you do this?"

"Don't you know? Can't you feel it?" Rafe made a fist, letting the power of the stone flow into his sister through the band around her neck.

"No. It can't be." She glared and snarled. "The Ankara Stone?"

Rafe nodded.

"How? How did you get the Ankara Stone?"

"Father gave it to me." His words dropped like a fallen god, making ever-widening ripples.

"Father gave…" Her voice trembled with heartbreak and envy, loss and betrayal. "And now it ends. Am I to die, then? Burned to dust, scattered on the seafoam? Swallowed by your precious ocean?"

"No. You don't end that easily, sister. Not after what you've done." Rafe sneered, ugly and bitter leaking past his words. "You will live, but not as you are."

Rafe met his sister's eyes and tapped the power of the stone once more. He felt the heat touch his skin, saw the shadow of the burning blue light against his eyelids, and heard his sister's frightened whimper. He watched her fade into unconsciousness and quickly retrieved her body from the sea.

He glided through the air, carrying her on board his ship. The crew kept their distance, but Mouse piped up, "Is she dead?"

"No, but incapacitated for now." Rafe laid his burden on deck. "I've temporarily repressed her powers." A strange looked crossed his face as he stared down at his sister.

She looks so peaceful. I've not seen her look like that in a long time.

"What are we to do with her?" The bitter voice of Hugh broke past his thoughts.

"For now it's the brig. The binding's not yet a permanent condition, so we'll arrange her a cell. I need to prepare some things before I eliminate her powers forever. Until then, we'll keep her on board, safely locked away."

"Aye, Captain." Blackthorne straightened his spine, and snapped, "Anders! Pinky! Down below and prepare a cell!" He sidled up to Rafe and whispered, "How long?"

In an answering murmur, the captain replied, "A day or two at worst. We have enough time."

Then he bent down and scooped up his sister, taking her below deck.

Chapter Twenty Two
Prisons

Hugh Corwin stood at the top of the steps leading to the brig, wondering if this was a good idea. Above him on deck, he could hear the sounds of victory and cleanup. He should be with the crew. No doubt, someone would notice him missing.

I've come this far. Might as well do it.

He walked slowly down the stairs, his boots clunking what seemed a thunderous echo on the wood. At the bottom of the steps he stood in the shadows. Afraid to venture farther. Part of him wished there was a guard on duty to send him away.

Hugh heard a scraping noise. Then a soft intake of breath and a faint giggle.

"Oh, my." A woman's breathy voice rippled the silence. "A visitor. Brother?"

Hugh didn't answer, wondering for the thousandth

time if he made a mistake. As he shuffled his feet, he heard a sniffing sound.

"No, not brother. Sailor. Come to see the prize? Show yourself."

Obeying, Hugh moved closer to the brig, drinking in his first close look at the Goddess of the Moon. His body trembled as anger and anguish warred in his soul.

She crouched in the cramped cell, her face contorted and her mouth drawn in a perpetual snarl, her fingers scratching at the binding spell around her neck. Her silver hair hung in tangles across her face and past her shoulders, and Hugh noticed tatters in the faded blue robes she wore. But somehow she still radiated a fierce beauty, and her essence shimmered light that both enveloped and illuminated the gloom below deck.

"Oh, a little ghost. Come to gawk. Stare, stare, little ghost. At the mother of your nightmares." She laughed, her face contorting into a rictus mask. "Gape and glare, get a good look. It might be your last. Or mine." She suddenly dug her fingernails into the wooden floor and gouged grooves in the boards. She lifted her fingers, bloodied, and laughed again.

"Does that hurt?" Startled, Hugh spoke without thinking, and it caught her attention.

She cocked her head, "Yes." For a moment her face softened. "But pain is reliable. I know pain. Pain and I are old companions."

Sudden misery bubbled up, and a faint melancholic sigh escaped him. "That I understand. Sometimes pain is all you have left."

A puzzled look bloomed. "What do you know of pain? You are dead. Your pain is done."

This time, Hugh laughed. A bitter and sour echo of everything taken away. "My pain started with my death. I lost everything. Alive, I had a new bride and a lifetime of hope and love. Now I have ash and what could have been. And knowing she'll live our life with someone else."

She scooted forward an inch or two, curious now. "You lost a love?" Her hand reached out, her fingers sliding against the cold metal bars. "A broken heart? Forever apart? How does it feel, little ghost? Tell me."

Hugh hesitated, and then the words poured out. "Empty. Pointless. Frightening. Like something vital was carved out of me with a dull knife." He balled his fingers into fists, not sure why he shared. "Sometimes I wish I'd been swallowed into oblivion, and other times..." His voice faltered, caught on emotion. "I keep thinking I can go back. Just go back."

"But you can't." She voiced his unspoken thoughts aloud.

That surprised him. He recognized something reflected in her gaze. His answer was quiet, laced with the pain of both their wounds. "No. I can't. I can never go back." Unnerved, Hugh turned to leave, but one more question forestalled him.

"How did you die?"

And the anger came back. Cold and deliberate, he looked at her and replied, "My ship went down. In a storm. One of your storms, I'm told." A small light of satisfaction lit his heart at her expression of shock. And a touch of regret. He left her without another word.

Rafe waited at the top of the stairs. "Did it help?"

"No." Hugh exhaled. A hollow sound following bitter emotion. "But it needed to be done." He pushed past the captain without another word.

Staring out at the water, listening to the mourning bellow of the sea monsters in the distance, Hugh admitted to himself that he lied to the captain. It had helped, talking to her. In an unexpected way, in a way that disturbed him. He felt sympathy for her. Briefly, fleetingly, but sympathy, nonetheless. For the great, terrible, Goddess of the Moon. For the fearsome deity that terrorized the Outer Islands and ruined his life.

How can I feel sorry for her? What is wrong with me? I should hate her. Revile her. But she... He let the thought trail off, hesitating for a moment to express it. *She's like me. She's in pain. I can't hate that. And I think... I think she still feels.*

"Hugh!" A shout interrupted his musings, and One-Eyed Anders strode up to his side. "There you are, lad. We're having a bash down below for Mouse, while the captain makes up his bloody mind on what to do with our new guest. Join us, I know our would-be hero would want you there."

Hugh smiled. "All right, I'll come." He followed Anders below deck grateful for the distraction. As they arrived, it became obvious that the celebration was in full swing. Quantities of beer, ale, and rum were flowing.

A shout went up at their arrival. "Grab an ale, boys, and celebrate our newest hero! Three cheers for Mouse!"

Anders grabbed a tankard as the hurrahs hit the air and Mouse blushed, but Hugh lingered near the door watching. He smiled and bantered when spoken to, and even gave Mouse a ruffle of hair and a cheery joke. His thoughts, however, strayed back to a goddess sitting in a darkened cell.

Hugh stayed half-past the hour and then slipped out from the party without a soul noticing. He made his way to the brig. He breathed a sigh of relief as he climbed down the steps to her prison, still unseen by any of the crew. He stood in the shadows, watching her by the glow of the flicking lantern hung on the wall. She sat in the centre of her cell, drawing invisible circles on the wooden floor.

"Have you come to gawk? Come to gloat?" She lifted her head and smiled, a strange, strained sneer. Her finger continued to make circles on the floor. "Oh, it's you."

"Yes. I don't know why I came." Hugh stepped into the

dim light. "I just knew I had to come. To talk to you again."

"Talk to me?" Surprise haunted her voice. Then she scowled. "Oh. To berate, accuse, denounce." Her finger stopped moving, and her hand closed into a fist.

"No. Just talk. You are not what I thought you'd be."

"Did you expect fangs?" She giggled, an almost childlike sound. "Maybe you thought I'd be eight feet tall?"

Hugh chuckled, despite everything. "No. Nothing like that." He took a breath and told her the truth. "I thought I'd hate you. Take one look at you and have a focus for my anger and pain. I never expect to feel sympathy."

She snarled. "I don't want your pity!"

"Not pity. A—a kinship, I guess. I look at you and I know. At least I think I do. I know the pain you feel. How alone you feel." Hugh took a step closer, and old feelings, old hurts spilled out, mixing in with his words to her. "I know what alone means. What a dark place it is. I know the look I see in your eyes. And I know you want someone to talk to, someone who will listen. That's why I'm here."

"Why would you do this? Such a thing? For me?"

"I—I don't know. Maybe you need it, maybe I'm tired of being angry. Maybe because someone did it for me. Maybe I just want to be kind."

"I am not used to kindness." The words drifted across the air slowly, harshly, in raspy tones.

The admission struck something in Hugh, a congruent chord. Kindness in abundance had not come his way either. Perhaps they *were* alike, all alone in the world. Still, she lived, unlike him. She had family, and the captain seemed to care. Sometimes. When the two of them weren't fighting. "Wasn't your brother, Captain Morrow, kind to you?"

"Captain Morrow, Captain Morrow. The great Captain Morrow." She rocked back and forth chanting his name. Then she looked up, her eyes wet, silver tears on her cheeks. "Yes, he was kind. Until the day it mattered most. I've wanted to hurt him for that. I did. It seemed simple. Just hurt him back." She stared, far past Hugh, far past the four walls of her cell. "But nothing is simple. Perhaps there was no kindness to be had then. Perhaps he... I am not sure anymore." She sighed, a faint puff of breath, like the night breeze on a calm sea. "And now, his kindness hurts too much."

"That I understand. Gentle words, helpful smiles that don't help at all. Surrounding you until all you want to do is scream."

She tilted her head, her brow furrowed. "Is that what I've been doing? Screaming? Monsters, monsters everywhere, screaming to the world?"

"Maybe. Lashing out to make everyone else hurt, too."

She leaned forward, scurrying closer to the cell bars. "That sounds like you've been having bad thoughts. Wanted to lash out."

"I did. I wanted to hurt the captain, the crew, every

person that couldn't see me. You." Hugh heard her faint gasp of breath, and flashed a wry smile. "Maybe it's a good thing ghosts can't do much damage."

"Not like gods." She cast her eyes downward.

"No, not like gods. But gods can stop destroying, you know. If they want."

She lifted her gaze. "Can they? Or is it too late?"

"You're looking at a man who died, but is still living, at least on this ship. Is anything too late in a world with such things?"

"Perhaps in the world of mortals. You are such ephemeral beings, sometimes so hopeful. I had forgotten that. Gods are more... stationary in their beliefs." She reached out and tapped the bar of her cell. "Like iron, we are. Rigid. Straight and tall, blind to all. Empty heads and empty souls. If we even have souls. Sometimes I wonder." She flashed Hugh a quizzical look. "Do you think I have a soul?"

Hugh nodded.

She giggled. "Wrong." She grabbed the prison bars, and swung back and forth, rattling the cage door. "No. No. No soul. Had one, now it's lost. Lost to the pain. Lost to the monsters. Lost to..." She stopped, sat quietly and folded her hands in her lap. "I listened to the darkness. To the caw of crows. Promises of worlds gone. Of my suffering obliterated. Promised the end of hope. End of all futures. Eternal oblivion. Make them all pay. Be the soulless destroyer." She smiled. "That's who I am."

"No." Hugh smiled back, tenacity and words tumbling out of his mouth. "No, and no again. People without souls don't feel pain. They don't feel anything. Your soul is lost. But not gone. And all lost things can be found."

She tilted her head as if pondering his words. "You are more mad than I, sir. Yes, mad, mad, mad."

Hugh laughed. "I may be. But I stand by what I said. Or maybe sit." He grinned and plunked himself into a seated position on the floor in front of the cell. "Whatever you are, you're not soulless. And despite everything, I like talking to you. Around you, I don't have to pretend."

"Yes. Talking is nice. I missed that. Nobody talks to me anymore. Except for my children. And they just grunt and scream and wave their tentacles. No conversation."

Hugh blinked and sucked in his breath, a shock shuddering down his spine. "Your children?"

"The monsters." She tapped her fingers across her knees. "Creatures only a mother could love. Sometimes. Yes, a sometimes love for my children. I do and I don't." She let out a sigh as wide as the sea. "I love them mostly, you know. They're not as bad as, well..." She shrugged. "You know. You've seen them. That's why I never love when the moon is full. No, not then." She fidgeted, running her hands along the wooden floor. "But I sing to them. When it's quiet, and the air is still. Pretty lullabies about the moon. The same ones I used to sing to your captain when he was a child. They always liked the lullabies." She started to hum. Softly, just under her breath. "Yes, they're good children when I sing."

"Are they just trying to please you? When they hunt in the moonlight?" The questions slipped out from Hugh's brain and past his lips without a coherent thought of what he asked.

She looked surprised, but not shocked or displeased. "I don't know. I never asked. Maybe. Maybe. Maybe they're good children doing bad things for their mother." She sighed again, an exhalation ripe with compunction. "It all got confused and jumbled. Puzzle pieces and pawns. Bits that don't fit anymore."

"Aren't we all?"

"Are you? A piece that doesn't fit?"

"Yes, I think I am. Maybe that's why I'm here. Looking to find where I fit. Hoping you know—" His words broke with a bang from above deck and a shout of his name.

"Hugh! Where you'd get to? Hugh Corwin!"

He scrambled to his feet. "I'd better go."

"Wait. Is that your name? Hugh?"

He nodded and disappeared into the shadows to rejoin the crew.

Chapter Twenty Three
Waning Moon

The break of dawn found Rafe watching the cherry tinted sunrise, a frown wrapped around his face. Few sailors were on deck, and all gave the moody captain a wide berth, for Rafe had no cheer for any of his crew this morning. He didn't even smile at the approach of familiar footsteps. However, he anticipated the question before asked. "It happens this morning, Blackthorne. Everything's prepared. Give the crew extra grog at breakfast. They'll need it."

"Am I getting that predictable, sir?" Not waiting for an answer, the first mate continued, "I'll let the cook know about the rations. Is there anything else you need me to do?"

"Dig some shackles out from storage. The crew will feel better if she's restrained when we bring her above deck."

"Aye, Captain," came the answer, followed by

retreating footsteps. Rafe contained another sigh but felt relief at being alone once more. Today was not the day he wished for company. No. Today was a day for mourning.

"You'll live, sister, but everything you were, and everything you are will cease to be. Who will you be tomorrow, I wonder? More broken than that shell of a creature in my brig, or free of your burdens?" He tossed a heavy exhalation into the sea. "I suppose it doesn't matter anymore."

The sound of voices made him turn his head. The crew had roused with tankards of grog in their hands.

The ever efficient Blackthorne. What would I do without him?

And with those thoughts, the captain went below deck.

After the morning meal, Rafe stood outside his sister's cell with shackles in his hand. "It's time, Manume."

"Is it? Time to go. Time to lose. Time to die." She giggled. "What is time, to us? Time, time, time. Never enough."

"Or too much. Too much time passed. Too much time lost."

She looked at him. "Has there been? Maybe, maybe. Too much of everything between us. Can't go back, can't go forward."

"Yes. We can only end."

"Will it? Or dangle like a fish? I don't know, I don't know. I think we are forever. Whatever we do." She sighed. "That's the tragedy."

"On that, we agree. We are a tragedy."

"So what now? Parade me in pomp and circumstance? Break me? Throw me to the fishes, and let them eat my soul?"

"You let me open the door and put these shackles on your wrists." He jangled the restraints. "Then we go up on deck."

Dutifully she did as her brother bid and allowed herself to be shackled and led topside like a docile spring lamb. Much of the crew had formed a loose half-ring around a double triangle rune Rafe had inscribed and imbued with magic on the quarterdeck planking. He walked his sister into the middle of the intersecting geometric shapes.

"A spell ward and binder. Is not this collar not enough?" She sneered.

"No. Not for what must be done. The power that must be unmade."

She stared into his face as if some horrid secret finally dawned. "You truly mean to do it, then? No taking me back, letting them deal with me? I die here today? Or do you castrate me, instead?"

"I'm making certain you stop hurting people. Hurting yourself. You've forfeited your right to be a god, sister. After today, you will no longer have that power."

"So, it's cut out all the bad bits and see what's left." She sneered. "Not much, I'd wager."

"And whose fault is that, sister?" A snatch of temper frayed through his composure. "You've brought this on yourself. I'm sick of pretending there's anything left of you to save. You're no better than your monsters that roam the sea. Devouring the innocent to feed your hate!"

She rocked back on her heels, silent, and Rafe pushed her down on her knees. She thrust her hands in front of her and rattled her chains. "Is this the part where I beg for mercy?"

"Do what do like. You always have." He turned his back and walked beyond the edges of the etched rune.

He took the Ankara Stone from an inner pocket of his coat, holding it in his palm. He took a breath, steadying his nerves for what he knew came next. He closed his eyes and recited the ancient spell.

"Dywch ar werc! Ymerch endr urd!"

The incandescent flash of light and the stone burned with a shining glow in his palm. He gritted his teeth against the pain he knew was coming as the stone again burrowed its way into his flesh and fused with his own innate magic. It took mere moments for the gem to disappear within his hand. He inhaled, enjoying its power coursing through him. He looked at his sister. She said nothing but smiled. A grin that said volumes in mockery and hate.

"So be it." He held up his hand, palm facing towards her. "Time to end it." Their eyes locked and he spit out the spell words. *"Indd demwys!"*

White energy marbled in blue spun from Rafe's hand and engulfed his sister, stabbing at her essence, connecting to her magic. She fell to her knees, her body pulsing in white and blue sparks, the runes on her arms glistening red like a bleeding heart. She shrieked her sorrow and her agony, a frenzied howl of the enraged and damned.

Undeterred, Rafe continued to recite the spell, *"Incean aryl andia, scryos andia."*

The sky quaked, the clouds turned crimson, and the ship shuddered as it bounced on the sudden roiling sea. The air snapped cold and dripped in bitter angst, wind smacking at the sails. Skin shivered, and sorrow seeped to the bone of every sailor standing on deck. A sorrow so profound that tears came unbidden to the eyes of the crew.

But her brother stood dry-eyed and maintained a stoic demeanour. Rafe remained still, his voice steady. *"Aganis, tosaionn, an deiradh."*

Manume screeched and for a moment the light of the perpetual moon above the ship wavered and dimmed. From the sea came responding screams. The heartbreak of monsters sailing on the prevailing winds.

Manume looked up and glared at him, hissing through clenched teeth, "My children know. They mourn." She bowed her head, only then noticing the vibrating shade of the runes. She raised her head again, slowly, and looked into the crowd, searching. She whispered, "Maybe gods can change, maybe they can't. But they need to be free."

Then she smiled and stared into her brother's eyes. "My children weep for their mother. They are dutiful creatures. They obey. They will do bad things for their mother. My children will do anything for me." She reached out slowly and placed a quaking hand on the wooden deck. "You made a mistake, brother. You forgot things. Things with black wings. And red runes that fight back." Her body shook and she moaned as the Ankara stone spell stabbed at her once more. But then she laughed, spewing out more words. "This ship is magic, brother dear. Magic. Magic is the key. I may not have my own, but I have his power, and I can use yours against you!"

Groaning and lashed with energy that drained her strength, she closed her eyes. Her lips moved, mumbling sounds, and the scars on her arms glowed a deeper red. A tendril of blue energy ascended from the core of the ship, snaking through her palm, and encircling her wrist. Where it touched her skin, the colour changed to scarlet. She jerked her hand upward and yanked the strand of magic free. She whipped it sideways, extending the now crimson power like a fishing line, out towards the sea. Then she screamed.

In an instant, her children bellowed a reply and leapt

from the water. The filament of energy grew and branched out, a dozen or more strands blossoming. The multiple lines of energy twisted around her creatures and ensnared a willing pack of sea monsters. Matter and bone, sinew and blood transformed into raw power and sucked down this lifeline of magic to the casting source: Their mother, Goddess of the Moon.

She glowed white hot and cherry-red, and her shackles shattered into chunks of flying metal. The binding glyphs painted on the deck seared to ash, and the collar around her neck dissolved in a flash of light. She let out a roar, a cry of anguish and triumph. The ship beneath her feet shuddered and heaved with an unrestrained assault.

"I am free and I will destroy you all!"

Chapter Twenty Four
Shipboard Battle

The stench of a newly-born lightning storm engulfed the ship, and the sizzle-snap of wild magic echoed along her lines. The *Jewel* shuddered again as if a giant fist squeezed her bones. Red radiance shimmied across the deck, and bolted up the mast, curling around the wood. The sails billowed in a shower of sparks and the smell of burning salt air.

"Your ship is mine!" Manume cackled and the ship rocked violently, rising on a sudden surge of tide and wave.

"Never!" With all the power of his magic and the Ankara Stone, Rafe punched his sister in the face, knocking her off her feet with an audible smack and a thump. She kicked out as she fell, but he sidestepped the blow. She used that moment to scramble upright, and then she charged at her brother.

A free-for-all fist-fight ensued. A screaming,

smacking, clawing, kicking, punching brawl, flashing feral energy and power around the open decks. Sailors ran, yelping and scattering for cover and fleeing below deck as the pair careened off post and stanchion, splintering wood and noisily flinging gear in their wake. The ship heaved, bucking like an untamed horse of the Outlaw Keys, its timbers groaning, adding to the sizzling, reverberating din of two gods at war.

"Did you really think you could best me, little brother? I'll tear you, your ship, your crew, and the worlds apart! I'll make you all pay!"

"Pay for what, sister? Your mistakes? Your inability to accept the fact that your human lover would die someday?" Rafe smashed a blue ball of energy and fury at Manume throwing her across ship into the fo'c'sle. He leapt after her, landing on the main deck.

"I warned you! I told you not to try! I told what would happen to him! Humans can't be gods! But you wouldn't listen! And we now all have to pay your folly? I'll never let that happen!"

"It was your fault! Yours! Why didn't you stop me? Protect him!" She screamed, a hellion of rage and lashed at him with a sizzling tentacle of magic. Rafe dodged, and it gouged a burn mark down the length of the deck. "You are the God of Souls! Why didn't you protect him! Him, of all people! You let him die!"

"You killed him! Face it, Manume! Your arrogance,

your belief that I was wrong killed him! You should have listened to me!"

Rafe roared the last words, the tenor and echo shaking the ship. They glared at each other, Manume at the fo'c'sle bulwark with the sea behind her back, and Rafe standing below, opposite from her. Between them ran the charred gash in the deck planking.

She whispered, "It's your fault," and lashed out, a line of scarlet energy arching towards her brother.

Rafe smiled and caught her makeshift whip in mid-flight before the blow could land. He yanked, and she yanked back sending a frisson of energy across the ship.

"A game, a game!" She cackled a trill of madness.

"This is no game!" A boom of anger reverberated and was answered with an abrupt *crack* and *snap*. The deck between them split. Rails shattered, and the ship shuddered, threatening to rip in twain.

Hugging the upper rail, Manume laughed again.

"Sink the ship! Sink the ship!" She pulled on her end of the energy strand only to be countered by her brother. "Who will win? Who will die? Maybe all!"

The shriek of wood and men's voices raised a din of bedlam as the ship shuddered and two gods battled for control. Blackthorne's voice sounded above it all, "What are you doing? Let go before we tear apart! Your magic is destroying us!"

The pair ignored him, as each vied to wrest dominance from the other. The widening crack separated brother and sister as each yanked on the magic tether in an ever-desperate tug-of-war. Between them, the ship shrieked like a beast being slaughtered. Around them, the crew shouted in terror and clung to whatever solid they could grasp as the vessel threatened to tear itself apart.

"Shall we shred this earth-bound ship and everyone on board? See how many die in the destruction and how many drown? I wonder if any of my children linger to gobble up the remaining souls?"

"You will not be alive to see that happen! I will kill you first!"

"No!" Hugh scrambled between them, dancing around the fissure and ducking the energy of the tether. Fear coloured his eyes wild and his voice shook.

Rafe snarled, "Get out of there! What are you doing?"

"This can't continue! You're going to kill everyone!"

Rafe hesitated, a slack in their tug of wills and magic. His vacillation reverberated down the energy and, in that same instant, Manume smiled. And then she let go, lunged forward, and leapt to the main deck.

Simultaneously, the backlash from the magic hit Rafe, knocking him off his feet, and his sister landed like a cat. She grabbed Hugh by the arm and yanked, narrowly dodging the split in the deck. The captain tumbled over broken wood and flying energy, scrambling to his feet in time to witness his sister jump from the ship, dragging Hugh with her. He raced to the rail and watched them both sink into the sea.

Chapter Twenty Five
Isle of Bones

Pulled under the surface of the water, memories exploded in Hugh's mind. Waves of expectation crowded all other thoughts. He remembered the night he died. The sensation of constriction, the choking, salty water filling his lungs, his thrashing desperation, and then the soft fading of awareness. Surrounded by the dark ocean, he anticipated it all again.

But nothing happened.

He calmly sank, the serene silence enveloping him. No end awaited him. No final fall into oblivion. Then he realized. The dead cannot drown.

The dead. Oh, no! The monsters! I have to get out of the sea!

Panicked, Hugh flayed his limbs and tried to swim to the surface. A rough hand reached out and yanked him farther below the water. Hugh fought the grip, jerking his head to see what held him.

The Goddess of the Moon smiled at him. She held a finger to her lips in a gesture of quiet. Hugh stopped struggling. She pulled him closer and took his hand in hers. Hugh closed his eyes as a soft red glow encircled them and they sailed away on the currents of the sea.

Far above them, chaos reigned.

"She's listing, Captain! Starboard! If she continues, we'll heave over! Whatever you're fixing to do, do it now!"

Ignoring the shouts and the frantic crew trying to keep the *Jewel* afloat and sailing, Rafe held the ship together by force of will. He poured the soul of his magic, fuelled by the Ankara Stone, into the frame and the vessel's life, knitting the broken structure back together fibre by fibre. Near human wails and groans echoed from the galleys and the darkest corners of the *Jewel* as if the ship suffered in agony. Slowly, sliver by sliver, board by board, the fractured ship became whole. She shuddered, shaking from prow to stern, and Rafe collapsed to his knees.

He put his hand on the deck and reached out with a touch of magic to assess the damage. He felt the ship's turmoil, a surplus of wounds, and sensed the uneven bearing, the listing of the hull.

Won't capsize, though, but she's low in the water. Flooded below decks. Damnation.

Rafe released the connection and lifted his tired head. He looked out at his home.

A strewn mess of broken wood and jumbled gear, mixed with torn bits of sail scattered the deck. The top of two masts were shattered, rigging and posts smashed into the prow deck and railing. Sailcloth flapped in tatters, and lines whipped free in the wind. Anders clung to the damaged wheel and the sailors who still stood manned their posts.

Rafe looked at them, the groaning injured, and the stalwart crew keeping to duty. He whispered, "What have we done?"

Hugh opened his eyes as light spilled down on his face. The black confines of the sea had vanished, replaced by the sand of a beach and the light of the moon.

"Awake, awake. Good."

Blue eyes stared at him from a pale face and a straggled, dripping mess of wet silver hair. The Goddess of the Moon smiled and waved her fingers at him.

"Get up. Get up. Not a lazy day. He'll be coming, coming."

Hugh sat up. "Who's coming?"

"My brother dear. Your captain, your wondrous Captain Morrow." She giggled. "He won't give up. Not him. Never, never, never." She jumped to her feet, standing over him and flapping her arms like a looming bird. "He'll swoop in on his ship, his ship." She stopped, suddenly still, and whispered, "We must prepare." She grabbed his arm and yanked him to his feet. She darted forward, pulling him behind her in a tumble of momentum and scurrying feet. They dashed along the sand following the shore. "We must prepare!"

Caught in her implacable grip, Hugh had no choice but to follow. He shouted, "Where are we going?"

"Home, home, we're going home!"

A few moments later, a structure both rounded and angular, a peculiar mess resembling a cross between a hut and a ship's prow, came into view. Manume halted, released his arm, and spread her hands in a wide gesture.

"Home!"

Awareness dawned in Hugh. "This is where you live?" She nodded. "That means this is... this place, this beach is part of..." A chill pierced Hugh's essence. "This is the Isle of Bones."

"Bones? Yes, yes, bones! Bones are what we need!" She spun about with a cackle and a dance step and then raced into her house. She quickly returned, holding a crescent-shaped amulet the colour of alabaster.

"Bones!" She spun around, laughing. "White bones. Red bones. Together, together. Fly high! In the sky! Like the crow. For Captain Morrow!"

She ran past Hugh waving her prize above her head. He hesitated and then sprinted after her. He caught up with her on the beach and stopped cold in his tracks. She was dancing. Across the sand. Her hair flowing, white energy radiating from her skin, arms glowing red and waving, feet shifting, spinning. And chanting, her voice shouting singsong words he didn't understand. Then realization dawned.

"Magic."

As his whisper melded into the air, the ground beneath his feet shuddered.

At the tremor, Manume stopped and whirled, a grin plastered across her face. She stared at him, and shouted, "They're coming!"

"How is she? Can the ship sail?" A haggard captain stared at Blackthorne.

"You tell me!" The first mate snapped back. "You know this ship better than anyone! Ask her!"

Rafe sucked in his breath, his expression etched in misery and regret. "I can't. She's angry. The ship will sail if she's able, but she won't talk to me. Won't tell me the damage." He sighed. "I know I was reckless, but my sister's still out there. With all her power restored and amplified. She's more dangerous than ever. We need to find The Goddess of the Moon."

"*Spit and damnat—*" Blackthorne bit off the curse, and continued. "Sometimes it's bloody hard serving on this ship, sir. But the bilge pumps are working and the flooding below deck is under control. We can get her operational within the hour, sir."

"Thank you, Blackthorne. I hope we have that hour."

"So do I." He turned as if to leave and then glanced back. "How are we going to find the goddess, sir? Are we going to traipse about aimless? She could be anywhere in these islands."

"No. I know where she headed. And that's the course we lay in, Blackthorne. Tell the men we are sailing to the Isle of Bones."

"Are you mad? We can't sail there! If the superstitions swirling around that place aren't sufficient to dissuade the crew, the harbours and inlets of that island are too treacherous! We'd never get close enough to lay anchor! You know that!" Blackthorne's ire fired again at Rafe.

Rafe whirled on his first mate and cast him a look that would burn the heart from any other man. Blackthorne stood his ground, if going a shade or two paler in complexion. Rafe held the look and spat his words out slowly. "I know nothing of the sort, Mr. Blackthorne. Only that I gave you an order, and I expect you to follow it. *To the letter.* Do you understand?"

Blackthorne straightened his spine, his mouth drawing close to a sneer as he replied, "Aye, Captain. Your orders will be executed. We head to the Isle of Bones."

"How much longer are you going to sit on the beach?" Hugh let exasperation and bewilderment creep into his voice. "You've been there for hours."

"I have. I watched the tide come in, go out. Got wet." She looked up at the perpetual moon. "Now I am dry."

"How long are you going to sit there?" Hugh sighed. "Can you at least tell me why? Why any of this?"

"Why? Why is irrelevant. You know why. He is coming. We must be prepared."

"Why isn't irrelevant! It might be pointless, but not irrelevant!" Hugh screamed, startling some seabirds into flight.

The Goddess of the Moon turned her head. "Pointless?" Her face looked confused.

"Yes, pointless. This whole fight. Pointless. No one will win anything. You and your brother are both doing it out of stubbornness and spite. Because neither of you will surrender, or apologize, or admit you were wrong."

"Pointless." In a low voice, she spun the word out like it was a gossamer thread on a loom. "Pointless. Pointless."

"Yes. I don't believe either of you tried to fix your problems. I'm not certain the thought ever entered your heads. Fighting was easier than facing your fears. Destroy,

destroy, destroy. No point, but fighting. And running from yourself. Like you can ever escape that."

"There I go, and here I am. Run, run, and never get away. That's what we do. That's what we all do."

"And does it ever work? Maybe you try stopping. Try standing still."

She shook her head. "That's when the voices whisper."

Hugh closed his eyes for a moment and then glared. "Maybe that's the problem. Maybe you need to listen to—"

"They're here!"

Hugh stared out at the sea. Indeed, a ship could be seen approaching, unmistakably the *Celestial Jewel*. "And so it starts all over." He spat in the sand. "I'll not stand here and watch!" He turned on his heel, but before a step could be made, Manume shouted, "Look!"

Hugh glanced back toward the ship. It had pulled up to anchor, sitting still in the water. Except the water wasn't there. At least in front of the vessel. He could see the captain standing on the jutting prow, glowing in blue magic. Before him, the ocean parted. Whatever spell he worked pushed aside the water as the tide sweeps debris to shore. Hugh stared at the shell and rock-covered sea bottom, watching in fascination as a few crabs scurried to find a new place to hide.

A shout broke the strange, silent scene. "Time to finish this, sister!" Rafe jumped from his ship, floating down between the suspended walls of water. As he walked to shore, the sea filled back into space he left behind. Soon, he stood on the beach. The tide nipping at his heels.

The Goddess of the Moon rose to her feet. She bowed to her brother, God of Souls. "One last fight. Winner takes the Worlds." She turned and glared at Hugh. "Go inside. Stay there." Hugh glared back but fled the beach for whatever safety her home provided.

She turned back. "Let's begin."

Chapter Twenty Six
Last Battle

Manume, great Goddess of the Moon, raised her crescent amulet above her head and laughed. Her cackling shriek raised itself to the sky and swirled the beach sand. Sparks snapped from Rafe's fingers in response and his eyes glowed a deep blue.

Manume then stuck out her tongue and screamed, "*Cyfodryrhyn!*"

The sky rumbled and a boom, much like thunder, split the air. The sea and sand quivered, the trees rustled, and a loud ceaseless rattle echoed from every corner of the isle. From grave and hollow, from shore and rock, they emerged, grotesque piles of bony remains fused with magic life. *Click, clack, click, clack,* misshapen skeletal creatures rising, moving, cavorting from their lost graves. This echo of clattering bones gathered along the beach to form a company of fantastic creatures, monstrosities ready to do battle.

"Do you like my new children?" She squealed her taunt with another mad bout of laughter following.

"No more than the old ones, sister!" Rafe shouted back in retort. "Let me show you mine!"

The blue sparks flickering off his fingers became flames. He gestured downward and the fire fed its way into the sand, snaking backward into the sea. The ocean danced with azure fire and glowed in sapphire. Waves undulated across its surface, shooting upward into waterspouts. Moans and the screech of the damned rode the cascades, and a host of ghastly spirits swept onto the shore to face the army of the Moon Goddess.

"Meet the Ghouls of the Sea, sister." An air-rupturing shriek sounded from the hoard of phantoms. "Drowned sailors condemned to an afterlife as denizens of the ocean. Angry souls, the unrepentant, unredeemed, rejected by the After World, doomed to an eternity trapped beneath the waves." Rafe smiled, a grin not of mirth, but of malice. "Some sent to their fate by your children, oh, Goddess of the Moon." Another shriek blew across the beach. "How shall we do this sister? Battle by sea or land?"

"Neither, brother! We take to the air! Ride the invisible stars and moonbeams! See where the fight goes from there!" With more laughter trailing her like lightning, she rose into the air fast as a storm wind, her grand legion of bones following her with rattling thunder.

"The sky it is then!"

Rafe chased her to the clouds on a streak of blue, leading the horde of angry screeching souls into war.

The sky erupted in a blaze of energy, cerulean and red-tinged pearl, a sizzling clash melding against the vaporous indigo heavens. A cacophony trumpet of sepulchral howls and cadaverous clatter became the thunder of the unfolding deity tempest. The moonlight faded against a sky erupting in light and colour, and the wind whirled a gale swooping down to bend the treetops and bounce the sea into waves.

"Show her your anger!" The booming voice of the God of Souls commanded his host, and his ghouls wailed the blood ravaging cry of the accursed undead. The bedlam discord surged like a hurricane breaker and smashed through her first line of bone creatures, striking the Goddess of the Moon with the full force of a tsunami. Flung above and past the island, chased by shards of skeleton, she skidded to a bloody dishevelled halt, but still primed for a fight. Below them, a ship rocked on the ocean, and a strange hut quivered with the echo.

"First hit, brother, but not good enough!" She shook her amulet with the force of the lunar tide and a fearsome growl spit from her throat. Crimson and ivory sparks spit from her mouth spinning into the bone shards from Rafe's attack. The fragments twisted on a whirlwind and hurled themselves back towards her brother, tiny arrows driving at his heart.

As sleek and fast as breath, five spirits moved to protect Rafe. Their ethereal mass became corporeal. Thunk after thunk, the shards embedded themselves in revived flesh. Then, in a lingering *whoosh*, solid became soul once more, and the impaled fragments fell to the sea below.

"Not good enough!" Rafe couldn't resist the taunt.

The Goddess of the Moon laughed. "Well played, brother! See how you fare against this!" She swayed against the clouds, swinging the crescent talisman. "*Dyrwich aei gulyd! Gened galeth Draic!*"

Streaks of white energy cracked over the sky—magic born lightning—hurtling down to pierce her army in a shattering explosion of bones. The sky danced with ruptured skeletons—a vast framework of the dead—soaring, twirling around their Goddess as if in a macabre ballet of subservience and worship. They veered and dove and merged in cracking jangles and snapping *thwacks* to arise all bone and patchwork and giant wings within the forever twilight sky.

Against the silver moon rose a flying beast.

A dragon of bones held together with silver and crimson magic.

And cackling, triumphantly riding on its back, silver hair blowing in the wind from its magic fuelled wings, stood the Goddess of the Moon.

"*Attack!*"

The great beast swooped across the gloomy sky,

chased by the sound of dying ships and falling stars, careening through the sea ghouls as if they were paper lanterns set adrift. Rafe spun upward in a tornado of blue fire, angled himself at his sister, and smashed into her in mid-flight. The pair rolled down the spiny back of the airborne creature, locked in a battling embrace. Then, with a flick of its tail, the immense monster flung them both backward. They tumbled apart, scrambling to their feet, facing each other in a conflagration of magic and hatred.

"No more emissaries! We end this between us!" Rafe slammed a blue flame at his sister, who dodged and stabbed at him with a white-hot blade of magic energy conjured from the depths of her being. The blow shattered on a hastily constructed shield, and he countered with a fireball that singed her hair as she jumped to avoid it.

Abruptly, the dragon banked left, chased by screeching sea ghouls, sending Rafe stumbling down its framework wing in whirligig manner to retain his balance. Manume fell, grabbing on to a protruding piece of bone to keep from plummeting off her beast. Rafe pitched a cobalt-hued fireball at her before tipping sideways from another soaring swerve. He tumbled, roars and howls in his ears, rolling along the wing to its edge. He slammed to a stop against a jutting ridge, fingers clutching it in a life-saving grip. The dragon dove and rose in a dizzying seesaw, banking a circle around the island, always keeping the sea beneath its course. From the corner of his eye, Rafe saw his ghouls in dogged pursuit.

He screamed, "Back away!" and the ghouls stopped chasing. The beast levelled its flight, content to fly loops around the isle as the sea ghouls watched.

Rafe scrambled to his feet and rushed his sister, mustering his magic as he ran. He blasted blue energy at her as she lunged forward. The pair crashed together in a surge of blue, white, and red combustion before lurching apart. Manume lashed out with her foot, kicking Rafe off his feet. He went down, striking his head against bone, stunning himself. He looked up to see his sister looming over him, and a blaze of white energy smashed into his chest. His body lifted, and his sister's power flung him into the back of the dragon's head. A shower of bone shards followed him, cutting into his flesh. Moaning, he rolled along the neck, smearing red specks in his path before returning to more solid footing.

Rafe rose to one knee, bloodied and battered, his left hand still ablaze with magic. His right hand steadied him against the dragon. "You could have finished me with that blow. Are you getting weak? Tired? Do your worst or surrender!" He stared, studying her, waiting.

Manume glared back, breathing heavily, but made no move to attack.

"What no follow-up blow? No clever words? Why haven't you ended me? You can't do it, can you?" Rafe stood, straightening to full height on shaky limb. His face was sad, bitter, and resigned. "But I can." He raised his hands, and summoned his magic, readying a decisive blow against his sister.

"No!" She screamed, and the cavernous echo shivered down the spine of the flying beast. Her hands shimmering in white light streaked with red. She dropped to her knees and smashed her fists and her amulet against her dragon. The creature quaked and cracked, fissures spreading like floodwater, splitting asunder in a roaring fracture of snapping bone. Any solid footing was lost as beast and magic disintegrated into light, dust, and shards. God and Goddess plunged into the ocean surrounded by a shower of bone and pursued by howling ghouls of the sea.

The force of hitting the surface slammed the breath out of Rafe's lungs, and jagged pain shuddered through his body. Dazed, he sank into the cold embrace of the water, watching the sparkling moonlight above recede farther and farther away. Around him, he heard moaning echoes muffed by the oppressing sea.

Close your eyes, and submerge.

For a moment, he nearly gave into the thought until his conscious brain, his survival instinct, kicked into gear. He flailed his limbs, struggling to swim, stroke after stroke, back up to the surface. His head broke into the clean, fresh air, and he gulped a deep breath of life and coughed briny liquid over his chin.

He glanced around. Bones floated in the water, scattered all about, but he saw nothing of his sister or his sea ghouls. A shiver raced his spine—reinforced as a faint scream reverberated below him—while the sea beside him boiled and exploded in a deluge of fluid and splintering magic. Chaos burst upward as the Goddess of the Moon ascended in a monumental struggle with the Sea Ghouls. She lashed out with fists, magic, teeth and scratching fingers as the ghouls swarmed her, shrieking, clawing with their reaching, grabbing hands. In moments, their numbers overpowered her and dragged her down into the black, frigid ocean where they lived.

As he watched his sister struggle and disappear, Rafe reacted on instinct, shouting, "Stop at once! I command it!" Sudden fear clutched at his heart and raced in his blood. "Bring her back!"

Brief silence held in eternity, then the sea erupted again, water spurting in a great funnel spray of aquatic liquid. Goddess and ghoul lifted far into the air, their entwined mass suspended for a moment, before the water dissolved into droplets beneath them, casting all in a descent downward. Manume fell without a sound, but the ghouls screamed still trying to reach her with grasping hands.

From the water, Rafe gave another shout, "Be gone!" And the ghouls vanished with angry howls. Only his sister struck the ocean swells and disappeared beneath the waves. Rafe dove after her, pulling her unconscious form back to the surface. Cradling her, he swam them both to the shore of the Isle of Bones.

Chapter Twenty Seven
Concord

Her eyes fluttered open. The Goddess of the Moon stared at her brother who knelt in the sand a few feet away. She eyed him with lingering suspicion and scowled. "Why did you save me? Why didn't you let them take me?"

Rafe hesitated and then said, "I don't know."

She continued to stare, the silence like an anchor weighing them down to the beach. Something rustled near the trees, and she glanced away. Turning back, she spoke. "Were you being kind?"

Rafe twitched, and an aspect of confusion spread over his face. "What?"

"Kindness." Hugh's voice sounded from the dunes above them "You remember that, don't you? You showed it to me once, so you're capable of it."

Rafe sighed. "Nice to know you're still among the living, Hugh. So to speak. I'm not sure what the both of you are talking about, but yes, maybe it was kindness. Or family bond, or memories, or one of a dozen things. I don't know. I just did it." He picked up some sand and let it run through his fingers. "I just didn't want you to die. Not like that. Not by their hand." He dusted off his palm on his trousers. "Maybe not at all."

The sound of the birds and the puff of the wind filled the silence. Hugh sat down on the grass, watching and waiting.

"You used to be kind." She spoke in a whisper, seemingly at no one in particular.

Rafe still answered her. "So did you. You had the most wonderful heart. I still remember that sister. I wish I still knew her."

"So do I. Sometimes. But that heart broke."

A soft wail came from the ocean, and the brother and sister looked out towards the sea, neither speaking, both knowing.

"So fix it." Hugh cut into the disjointed quiet. "Fix what's broken. Keep talking. Stop fighting."

The sighs of two deities sailed to the clouds on the sea wind. They stared at each other but said nothing. Hugh threw his hands up and groaned, kicking grass and dirt in frustration. Then he rose and walked away.

Rafe's mouth quirked a half-smile. "I think he's mad at us."

Manume nodded. "He does things like that. He's

very strange." She sat up, curling her arms around her knees. "I like him, though. He's nice. Tells me the truth."

"Humans don't do that often, do they? Tell us the truth. They're usually too afraid or awed."

"They run. They all run. Run, run. So afraid. I'm a terror." She giggled. "He didn't run."

Rafe tilted his head. "He didn't seem intimidated by me either. Rare that."

"Maybe he's just too stupid."

Rafe chuckled. "Maybe. Or too stubborn."

She lowered her eyes and watched a tiny crab crawl on the sand. Then she whispered, "Maybe he's too clever. Sees through us."

"Maybe." Rafe reached out a hand, and she met it with her own. Their fingers closed and entwined.

They sat on the beach watching the crab, holding hands, and saying nothing. Above them, the sky sparkled a velvet blue, and the stars and moon shone a pearl light on the calm sea.

Two shadows fell across the silent pair: one from the dunes. One from the shore side. They looked up. A quizzical Blackthorne and an irritated Hugh looked back.

"Sir, we were wondering, is it over?"

"Yes. Are you done trying to kill yourselves and

wreak havoc?" Hugh snapped his question like a crab defending itself.

Rafe looked back at his sister. "Are we? I think I'm done. What about you?"

She cast down her eyes, drawing little circles in the sand with a free finger, but she didn't let go of her brother's hand. "It all comes round and round, like the moon when it's full. So big, so bright. Sometimes blinding. Best choice. Only choice? Yes. No more killing. No more mad."

"So now what? We all walk away." Blackthorne's query fell like rain after a storm.

"I—I don't—I," Rafe sputtered, stumbling over indecision.

His sister looked up, straight into his eyes. "Are you going to take my powers away?" The words came out soft and low in the cadence of a frightened girl.

Rafe squeezed her hand. "I should. It's what I planned. You know that." She nodded. "But somehow it doesn't seem right anymore." He sighed. "Yet, I can't leave you like you are, either." He shot a glance at the runes on her arms.

"No. Not a good idea. Too tempting."

"So what do we do?"

A quiet cough, a clearing of the throat interrupted, followed by, "Perhaps, sir, a compromise?"

Rafe gave his first mate a sideways glance. "Speak up,

Blackthorne. What's on your mind?"

"Well. I am unsure how these sorts of things work precisely, but might a limitation on her powers be possible?"

The siblings exchanged a look, and then Rafe smiled. "As always, Blackthorne, yours is a voice of practical solution." Another glance between brother and sister. "It could work, if you're willing."

She nodded again. "A little left, a little gone. I can accept that."

"Shall we get started, then?"

The pair scrambled off the sand and walked farther down the beach. They stopped when they were just out of sight of the others, facing each a few feet apart.

Rafe spoke first. "I won't need the binding spell this time, I take it?"

"No. I won't fight it."

Rafe outstretched his arm, palm up, feeling the cool breeze on his skin. He summoned the magic of the Ankara Stone still embedded inside his hand, and a blue-white glow spun upward in dancing filaments.

"Ooh, pretty. Like my children's tentacles."

Rafe suppressed a smile and continued. The magic grew, the threads reached out and wrapped themselves around the Goddess of the Moon in a latticework cocoon.

She laughed. "It tingles."

"That may not last." Sadness reflected back to her.

"I know." She smiled at him. "Finish it."

"Torilri'r sylltiad au a rhwym rhud! Eth uwaith yngryf, ynawr yngwn! Udwan! Rhwch! Hannery perhiyn medd uydd wiesh!"

The filaments surrounding his sister flashed and shimmered, bursting in fresh energy from the spell. She screamed and fell to her knees as the binding did its work, slowly melting into her flesh. Energy swarmed inside, threading through her blood and sealing a great part of her vast power—old and new—behind a woven lock of magic. When the spell finished, the cocoon was gone, and her skin was covered in cerulean coloured tattoos. Any trace of the red runes vanished from her arms.

Rafe knelt beside her. "How do you feel?"

She looked up. "Less. Better."

"It worked, then?"

She nodded. Then she stared at her hand, turning it over to view the artwork etched there. "Pretty. Better than the last time. I don't like ugly scars."

"A side effect of the spell. A visual manifestation of the binding."

She shrugged. "Still pretty."

"Yes." Rafe helped her to her feet. "Shall we return to the others?"

"Wait." Manume leaned in and whispered in his ear. "A warning, brother. I was not alone in this. You needn't fear me any longer, but beware the Nightmare Crow. He is not finished with you." She rocked back on her heels and smiled. "Now we can go."

Ignoring the questions written in Rafe's expression, she walked past him and headed back up the beach to Hugh and Blackthorne. Her brother shrugged and followed.

A pacing pair awaited them. "It's done." He saw relief on their faces but said nothing. He turned to his sister instead. "Is there anything you need to tell me? More secrets regarding birds, perhaps?"

She tilted her head and giggled. "No. No. No. Little bird, nasty bird. Its secrets are not mine to tell. No, not mine." She spun around with another laugh.

He sighed, but with a smile. "Very well. With that, I should most likely take my leave, sister, but I hope we see each other soon."

"We will, I think. A happier meeting next time." She moved suddenly, and Rafe found himself engulfed in a hug. He smiled and returned her embrace. It only lasted a moment but bridged monumental years of separation.

With their goodbyes said, Rafe turned to Corwin. "Well, Hugh, time to leave this place and set sail. We can finish your journey to the After World as soon as I reopen the portals."

"No, sir. I'm staying here."

The Goddess of the Moon whirled to face him. "What? Why?" Surprise sliced through her tone, mixed with some suspicion.

"Why do you think? Someone has to keep an eye on

you. It might as well be me." He shrugged, threw up his hands, and stomped away across the dunes. Manume watched him go, humming a little tune.

"You're right, sister. A very strange man indeed." Amusement tickled Rafe's voice.

"Strange, strange, very strange. I like that."

"Well, he can stay, if you want him."

She smiled. "I want him."

"That just leaves us, Blackthorne. Back to the ship and set sail for the Outer Islands."

"Aye, Captain."

Chapter Twenty Eight
Ebbtide

The *Celestial Jewel* sailed calm open water towards the Sea Portal as the sun settled well past the noon apex, lighting the sky in a warm burst of light. The affairs of gods, the Sea of Perpetual Moon, and the Archipelago of Nightfall lay in their wake, and the mood of the crew sparkled buoyant and jolly. The captain and his first mate stood at the rail watching the ship cut through the water, and listening to the flap of the sails overhead. A seabird soared with the prevailing winds, trailing along the edge of the ship, before veering off and heading inland.

"It almost feels as if nothing happened. Now." Blackthorne's calm voice cut the silence in half. "But things will change now, won't they?"

"They will. Somewhat. The nights of full moons won't always mean storms and death, though we'll still have our duty when the ships go down. And there are still monsters out there. Not every foul sea creature met its demise by its mother. They'll still be a menace, I think, though perhaps not as much."

"Does that mean the towns and seaports are still in danger?"

"Doubtful. That was her doing, and... whatever augmented her magic. The beasts should go back to their natural instincts. Feeding on ships and sailors. The seas are still a place where monsters roam, Blackthorne."

"And what of this other thing, sir?"

"We have a name, now. At least she gave me that much. The Nightmare Crow."

"Well, that doesn't sit well. Conjures to mind dark trouble, that name."

"Indeed. I fear we've more trouble on the horizon in regards to that, my friend." He sighed, then the edge of his mouth quirked. "But not today. Today, that is not our concern. Today, we restore the Sea Portal and the balance between the living and the dead."

"I'll be glad of that as will the rest of the Outer Islands and The Seven Kingdoms. Perhaps then we can have some shore leave."

"Not quite yet. Tomorrow's task is still ahead."

"What's on the roster for tomorrow, sir?"

"A trip to the Isle of Shadows. We have to return this to my father." He slipped the Ankara stone from a pocket, gave it a toss in the air before catching it and returning to the dark folds of his coat.

Blackthorne watched the show with a groan. "Oh, the crew will love that piece of news."

Rafe smiled. "Won't they just. But that's tomorrow's problem. Let's simply enjoy the day, shall we?"

"Aye, Captain. Aye."

The pair smiled, as a shadow passed over the sails. Far above the ship, a crow flew on black wings and rage.

Book Extra

Here's the original piece of flash fiction I extended into this novel.

Ghosts of the Sea Moon

The moon blended into the obsidian sky, a luminescent silver veneer striding across the horizon. Its grace swayed and suspended on shifting ethereal clouds. Its children stars gathered close within a bright, shimmering embrace. To the melancholy sailor on deck, the lunar object seemed to be the ship's destination, the full sail and choppy wake speeding the vessel to the heavens.

"She's a sight, the Sea Moon. Once a year, she looms vast and grand above us, beckoning home her seafaring brood. But she'd swallow us whole if we let her."

The sailor flinched, the captain's voice abrupt and loud in his ear. The man gave no warning to his presence for the ship's master had a step as quiet as a cat's paw.

"Do you really think it would swallow the ship, sir?"

"Aye, in a fashion. Not the moon itself, mind you, but the celestial magic spilling into the air and sea. And it could do worse if we miscalculate the bearings. It's tricky work navigating these moonbeam waters and the otherworldly rifts." The captain smiled and clapped a hand on the sailor's shoulder. "But not to worry, lad. I've been doing this run a long, long time, and I never floundered my ship in the hoary moon mist yet. I'll get you home."

"Home." The sailor let the word flop on his tongue, its taste bitter. "Home is far behind this ship, back on shore with a weeping widow who barely had time to be a bride."

"Aye, lad. I'm sorry for what you've lost, and the hardship of your death. I hope you take some comfort in the fact that I plucked your spirit from the deep before the sea demons feasted on your soul. Moreover, be glad you finally accepted your fate. Some never leave this ship, vainly hoping to find a way back to the living." A fleeting frown crossed his lips and then pivoted back to his customarily, wry smile. "Besides, my lad, you'll see your widow bride again one day, in the afterlife you're seeking, and there'll be people who went before you waiting there for you. So be cheered."

The sailor said nothing, simply turned his face to the imposing moon as the ship of ghosts sailed toward his last port of call.

Pronunciation Guide

Manume – pronounced Man-You-May

Cylla, – pronounced Sill-Ah

Lynna – pronounced Lin-Ah

Aryna – pronounced Are-EE-Na

Reis – pronounced Ray-iss

Bevire – pronounced Bev-ear

Abersythe – pronounced Ab-Er-Sigh-th

Llansfoot – pronounced Lans-foot

Amaratha – pronounced Am-Ara-Tha

Kyyn – pronounced Kin

List of Gods in the Book

Captain Rafe Morrow, God of Souls

Goddess of the Moon (Manume)

Cylla, Keeper of the Gate in the Isle of Shadows

Lynna, Goddess of the Sea

Aryna, Goddess of the Wind

Reis, Sovereign of the Gods

Bevire, Goddess of Shadows and Night

Also in the series

Souls of the Dark Sea
Renegades of the Lost Sea